Nessie's Nemesis

By Chris Chan

First edition published in 2023
© Copyright 2023 Chris Chan

The right of Chris Chan to be identified as the author of this work has been asserted by him in accordance with the Copyright, Designs and Patents Act 1998.

All rights reserved. No reproduction, copy or transmission of this publication may be made without express prior written permission. No paragraph of this publication may be reproduced, copied or transmitted except with express prior written permission or in accordance with the provisions of the Copyright Act 1956 (as amended). Any person who commits any unauthorised act in relation to this publication may be liable to criminal prosecution and civil claims for damage. All characters appearing in this work are fictitious. Any resemblance to real persons, living or dead, is purely coincidental. The opinions expressed herein are those of the author and not of MX Publishing.

Hardcover ISBN 978-1-80424-242-1
Paperback ISBN 978-1-80424-243-8
ePub ISBN 978-1-80424-244-5
PDF ISBN 978-1-80424-245-2

Published by MX Publishing
335 Princess Park Manor, Royal Drive,
London, N11 3GX
www.mxpublishing.com

Cover design by Brian Belanger

Once more, to my parents, Drs. Carlyle and Patricia Chan.

Thanks for everything.

And to Mr. John Stephens ("J.S.") and Prof. Carolyn Stephens, for their encouragement.

TABLE OF CONTENTS

Chapter 1 - The Happiest Place in Scotland	1
Chapter 2 - The Missing Monster Hunterz	18
Chapter 3 - The Leading Writers of Their Time	49
Chapter 4 - The Police Have Questions	76
Chapter 5 - Lunch and the Blame Game	91
Chapter 6 - Peerage Maker	120
Chapter 7 - The Guests are Fleeing	145
Chapter 8 - The Great Sausage Scandal	169
Chapter 9 - Voyage to the Bottom of Loch Ness	191
Chapter 10 - All the Answers	208

CHAPTER ONE
The Happiest Place in Scotland

"So Addy, explain to me again how Sherlock Holmes is connected to the Loch Ness Monster."

I suppose I hadn't done a very good job of describing the letter I'd received that day. My girlfriend Zabel was justifiably confused. Admittedly, I was talking a bit fast. I was rather excited about the prospect of going to Loch Ness. I'd always wanted to see it, but I'd never gotten around to making the journey. "Perhaps I'd better show this to you."

She accepted the letter I pulled from my coat pocket and unfolded it. As part of my work, I receive a lot of odd items in the post. It's all part of the job when you're Sherlock's Secretary.

That's not my official title, but it's what I tell people I do for a living. In Sir Arthur Conan Doyle's Sherlock Holmes mysteries, the great detective lived at 221B Baker Street until he retired and moved to Sussex to raise honeybees. In real life, there's no private residence at that address in London, but instead, there's a bank. For decades, people have been sending letters to 221B Baker Street addressed to Sherlock Holmes, and the post has delivered them to the bank.

There are multiple ways of dealing with this situation. The bank could write "Not known at this address" and return them to the Royal Mail. Alternatively, the letters could be tossed in the bin unopened. But people who write to Sherlock Holmes are often in dire situations, and they're desperate for help. You can't just ignore them.

So the bank realized that somebody had to reply to the letter-writers. There've been several people who've filled the position over the decades, and not long ago, I was hired for the job.

I should point out that it's not one of my responsibilities to actually solve people's problems. If someone writes with a crime to solve or something like that, I don't pop a deerstalker hat on my head, pick up a magnifying glass, and go out and investigate. At least, not most of the time. I am not a licensed inquiry agent. The best I can do is refer them to actual private investigators or Scotland Yard. Of course, not everybody writes regarding a mystery. Some people just want Sherlock Holmes' autograph, or a signed photo of one of the actors who's played the part. I can send the latter requests along to the actors' personal assistants, though in some cases, such as if it's a young child who wants Sherlock Holmes to be a pen pal, I assume Holmes' persona and reply.

It's an enjoyable job, especially for a fan of mysteries like myself, and it was all pretty low-stress until several months ago, when a couple of bank robbers broke into my office and stole some letters addressed to Sherlock Holmes. I met Zabel in the wake of that burglary. She makes her living as an independent true crime reporter. When the police weren't that interested in pursuing the case, the two of us started digging around and eventually found out the reason for the theft. We wound up telling the story on social media, and I even wrote a book about the case, and it made us minor celebrities in the true crime world. It led to me getting a lot more mail at the bank, including the following letter:

Dear Mr. Zhuang,

        Hello! I'm writing to you from Inverness, Scotland. As a fan of Sherlock Holmes, you are no doubt familiar with the Inverness Cape, and also how the most famous body of water in the general vicinity, Loch Ness, is connected to the 1970 Billy Wilder movie "The Private Life of Sherlock Holmes." Assuming you've seen that movie, you know that a critical plot point focuses on the Loch Ness Monster and a government secret. When Wilder was filming the movie, he made a change to the design of the Loch Ness Monster prop, which led to it sinking to the bottom of the Loch. The long-lost prop was recently rediscovered several years ago, but for a while now, some people have tried to have the "head" of the "Loch Ness Monster" raised from the bottom of the deep. Last week, a couple of young enthusiasts attempted to retrieve the head, but they both disappeared mysteriously. We're not sure what happened to them, but we don't believe that they drowned, as no empty boat was found on the water, and all of their diving equipment was left in their hotel room. The local authorities have found some notes in their room connected to the film "The Private Life of Sherlock Holmes," but their journals have a ton of references that only a Sherlock Holmes expert would be able to understand. As a fan of Miss Carvalho's videos, I thought of you, and I hope that you can come here to help us with our questions, please. Thank you!

    Sincerely,
    Senior Constable Pherson Waldroup

I followed Zabel's eyes as she read the letter twice, and as she handed it back to me, I could see the familiar glow in her face as the first twinges of excitement over the start of a new investigation.

"What do you think?" I asked.

"I'm willing to take a trip to Loch Ness if you are! Will the bank give you time off?"

The bank would and it had. The moment after I asked my supervisor for a few days of paid leave, he responded with a hearty approval, and even offered me a modest– actually spartan– per diem to cover expenses, at least partially. Ever since our successful resolution of the bank robbery case, my work answering Sherlock's Holmes' mail had brought a lot of positive attention to the bank, leading to a lot of new customers depositing their savings there. Apparently linking your institution with Sherlock Holmes can earn you a lot of good will and positive press. Before my big adventure several months earlier, I had spent my entire working day in my office, rarely seeing anybody else except for the occasional tourist who heard about my work and wanted to see my collection of Holmes-related memorabilia. But even on a busy day, there's rarely enough letters in the post to take up more than a few hours of writing, leaving me plenty of time to read and work on my own writing projects. But sometimes notoriety brings unexpected responsibilities, and my boss has gotten into the habit of sending me out to give presentations on Sherlock Holmes at libraries and schools, and perhaps the odd literary conference, all to drum up more publicity for the bank.

All my boss asked in return was for me to write a bunch of blog posts on my adventures for the bank's website. Despite the fact that he used a generous amount of terminology and buzzwords that I didn't understand, I could follow enough of his train of thought to realize that the response to my Sherlock Holmes-related work had been positive. For the life of me, I couldn't understand how getting likes on social media benefited a financial institution, but as I was getting what I wanted, I figured my best course of action was to smile and take the win.

Zabel's her own boss, so she didn't have to ask anybody else for permission to take a trip up to Scotland. We booked a couple of rooms at a little hotel in Inverness, filled up the tank of Zabel's car, and prepared for our newest adventure.

The next morning, I was packed and ready for the trip, and waiting for Zabel. I live in a nice little flat in London that I can only afford because I share it with my two best friends from university. Sanna Mahabir is a solicitor, and as she never stops reminding us, she's the only one in our small circle of friends with a traditional, responsible job. Jasper, in contrast, is a YouTuber who talks ad nauseum about popular culture trends that annoy him. Amazingly, he manages to make more money than me and Sanna combined, much to Sanna's blind rage. How it works I couldn't tell you, but hats off to him to find a way to make a decent living without ever having to leave the flat.

"How long will you be gone?" Sanna asked.

"I don't know for sure. It takes about a day to get up there and a day to get back, so let's say at least three days. Not more than five. Are you going to be O.K. being alone with Jasper for that long?"

"I haven't seen much of him lately. He's been hosting all of those livestreams lately with his friends from all over the world, ranting about how superhero movies aren't as super as they used to be, and why Hollywood executives don't have a clue about how to write male heroes anymore. I can't believe that people watch them talk for four hours and drop cash into his digital tip jar."

"Speaking of work, how's yours going?"

"There's a potential storm on the horizon. I can't go into details, but I suspect that one of our biggest clients may not be on the up-and-up. If I'm right, I'll be sifting through files non-stop. If I'm mistaken in my suspicions, if I pace myself, I might be about to have a bit of a holiday myself this week. I may try that new curried ice cream shop on the corner. Catch a film or two."

"Sounds like fun. Let's hope you're wrong about that client. Any plans for meals now that I'm not going to be around to cook?"

"Darn it, it's too early in the morning for me to plan any meal more complex than pouring puffed rice in a bowl and adding milk. Maybe I'll take a page out of Jasper's book. The man survives on delivered pizzas and kebabs."

As I glanced out the window, I saw Zabel driving up in front of the building, so I said a quick goodbye, grabbed my suitcase, and hurried downstairs. We didn't talk much until we had cleared the London traffic, but once we reached the open roads of the countryside, Zabel relaxed and was once again ready for conversation.

"So Addy, I was going to do a little Internet research last night, but I got caught up with packing and forgot. What is this *The Private Life of Sherlock Holmes* movie that was mentioned in the letter?"

"All right. Are you familiar with the films of Billy Wilder?"

"Mmm..."

"*The Lost Weekend? The Apartment?* Both of those won the Best Picture Oscar, in the mid-1940s and early 1960s, respectively."

She sighed. "Don't look down on me for this, but I really haven't seen that many movies from before I was born. I'm not proud of it. It's not that I have a problem with old movies, not like my youngest sister, who won't stop sniping about how she refuses to watch black and white films. Again, that's not how I feel – " Zabel must've read my face, and she responded so hurriedly I wondered if she was worried I was going to break up with her due to incompatible taste in entertainment. Trust me, that would never happen, but it's nice to think that was a fleeting concern, especially because, as Sanna never tires of reminding me, at least in conventional terms of physical attractiveness, Zabel is way out of my league.

"– But I've just never gotten around to watching many classic films," Zabel continued. "I know that's more your field. Can you give me a little more background on *The Private Life of Sherlock Holmes?*"

"Sure. First, Billy Wilder is one of the legends of Hollywood. He was nominated for tons of Oscars for directing and screenwriting, winning six times. Lots of actors in his films got Academy Award nominations and wins as well. He worked in a lot of different genres, like film noir. Did you see *Double Indemnity?*"

"No. Please don't judge me."

"I'm not. He also made classic screwball comedies, like *Some Like it Hot*."

"That's the one with cross-dressing, right? With Dustin Hoffman?"

"You're thinking of *Tootsie*, Zabel. But yes, that one has Jack Lemmon and Tony Curtis on the run from the mob, pretending to be women, and Marilyn Monroe's in it, too. He also worked in the courtroom drama genre, with Agatha Christie's *Witness for the Prosecution* – we saw the play at London's County Hall a couple of months ago."

"I remember. That was really good."

"And he also did the classic Hollywood tragedy *Sunset Boulevard*."

"I saw the Andrew Lloyd Webber musical with my parents years ago. But I get it, he worked in a lot of genres. And he liked Sherlock Holmes, too?"

"Yes. *The Private Life of Sherlock Holmes* was one of his last films, which he co-wrote, directed, and co-produced. He'd wanted to make a Sherlock Holmes musical for years, but the studios didn't like that idea, so he wound up jettisoning the songs and writing this original screenplay, which is not based on any of Sir Arthur Conan Doyle's original stories. Interestingly, the movie was meant to be a massive epic, filled with mini-mysteries and running nearly three and a half hours long. But the studio acted as the stereotypical Hollywood studio does, and decided it was way too long, so they sliced and diced over an hour of the film, and a lot of the mini-mystery scenes are considered lost – pretty much nothing but the audio remains from those forcibly deleted scenes. A lot of film buffs dream of someday discovering the lost footage, but it's unlikely it exists anymore."

"It sounds a lot like our investigation into the BBC's 'Great Erasure' when we first met," Zabel noted.

"Exactly. Anyway, all that remains is an opening narrative where a Russian ballerina wants Holmes to knock her up and create a superkid with her looks and his brains, and Holmes is only able to get out of it by insinuating that he and Watson are a couple, which mortifies Watson. Most of the movie is devoted to the search for a beautiful woman's missing husband. The case leads them to Loch Ness, where they actually see the monster, but it turns out that it's a super-secret submarine in disguise, and it's all overseen by Holmes' brother Mycroft as part of his work for the British government. Anyway, by the end, spies are uncovered and Holmes is emotionally wounded. That's a pretty oversimplified summary, but that puts the meat and potatoes on the plate."

"That it does. We'll have to watch it sometime."

"I brought the DVD with me. We can watch it on my laptop later, if you like."

"Sure. But what about that sunken Loch Ness Monster replica that was mentioned in the letter?"

"Oh, that. That's a legendary lost prop. You see, when they were filming the movie, they needed to create a fake Loch Ness Monster head for scenes where the main characters see the supposed creature, seen gliding through the water."

"Was it motorized?"

"No," I replied. "I'm pretty sure that it was towed by a boat, though the rope was kept just below the surface of the water, out of sight from the camera. Originally, a portion of Nessie's body was visible in addition to the head, like a couple of little curves in the body just sticking up out of the water. But for whatever reason, Wilder didn't like the look of it. So he ordered the curves removed. The production team warned him, saying that smoothing down the body would throw off the balance of the model, but Wilder insisted. So they tried out the new version, and moments after they started testing it, the off-kilter Nessie wobbled, and sank to the bottom of the loch. There's no record of whether or not the designers told Wilder "We told you so.""

"How big was this Nessie model?"

It took a few moments to dig that information out of the crevasses of my brain. "I think that it was about thirty feet tall. Anyway, it turns out that Loch Ness is not the best place to film on location anyway, as the lighting just wasn't right. So they wound up building a new, more stable Nessie, and they filmed it in a water tank on a studio set, and that worked."

"And they didn't try to pull the sunken model out of Loch Ness?"

"I guess not. Maybe it would have been too expensive or something like that, or they didn't have the necessary diving equipment. They'd probably have needed a crane to get it out of the water, anyway. So, long story short, when the film crew packed up and left, the Nessie model stayed behind, and it was considered a lost prop for about half a century, until somebody with a waterproof robot started poking around, and eventually found it at the bottom of the loch."

"Any plans to have it removed?"

"Not as far as I know. You would think some movie memorabilia opportunists might go after it, but as far as I know nobody's tried to haul it out of the water and put it in their swimming pool or something like that. It's so big, anyway, it's not like people can just tuck it in their pockets and slip away, whistling casually."

My mobile chimed, and I fished it out of my coat pocket and checked it.

"Something wrong?" Zabel asked.

"It's my Mum. I talked to her last night, and there was something… off about her tone. I had to carry most of the conversation, and when I asked her if there was something on her mind, she prevaricated a little while and told me not to worry. I texted her this morning to check and make sure that all was well, and she just wrote back to assure me that everything is fine, and she has some news for me – all good, nothing to fear – but she can't tell me for a few more days."

"Why not?"

"She didn't say."

Zabel took her eyes off the road just long enough to assess my expression. "Are you worried?"

"More perplexed than stressed out, really. If something truly horrible were happening, then Mum would let me know. It's just… odd. She's being rather secretive, and that's not like her at all. Normally Mum tells me everything that's going on, from what she had for breakfast to the latest movie my siblings watched."

We were silent for a while, and then Zabel made the terrific suggestion that perhaps we ought to listen to music, and that took the place of conversation for the next couple of hours. Zabel gave a reasonably solid performance singing along to most of the songs, and I hummed along whenever I was familiar with the tune. Shortly after noon, we had a quick lunch at a fish and chicken shop, and for the rest of the journey we discussed plans for refining the next three entries in Zabel's latest video series, a six-part documentary covering the Bravo Poisoning Case of 1876, and we brainstormed over how to present how that crime exemplified problems women faced during that era without coming across as being too preachy.

The discussion absorbed so much of my attention that I completely lost track of time, and just at the meeting of afternoon and evening, I saw a sign informing us that we had arrived in Inverness.

"Did you know that Inverness was ranked as the happiest place in Scotland?" Zabel asked.

"Not until last night, when I did a little background research on the city. I wonder what it is that makes it such an upbeat place."

"Perhaps there's something in the waters of Loch Ness that boosts people's spirits."

I smiled, as a similar theory had crossed my mind, but Zabel had beaten me to the quip. After putting the return address from Senior Constable Waldroup's letter into the directions app on my phone, we followed the instructions for ten minutes before arriving at the station.

"I hope we're not too late. What happens if the senior constable went home for the day?" I wondered. "Will they give us his home address, or maybe his phone number? Or will we have to come back tomorrow?"

Stifling a yawn, Zabel said, "After all that driving, I'm totally fine with being forced to go to the hotel. I'm probably going to need to go to bed right after a shower and dinner."

The station was a rather imposing-looking building that made me feel relieved that I was entering as a willing volunteer there to help the authorities, rather than as an accused criminal. After checking with the front desk, it turned out that Senior Constable Waldroup hadn't gone home for the day yet.

After going the wrong way down the hall twice, we finally found the right door and knocked. The muffled "Come in!" suggested to me that Waldroup's mouth was full of food, and as I opened the office door and looked inside, a glance at the half-eaten, rather sad-looking fast-food hamburger sitting on a greasy wrapper suggested that my guess was correct.

"Yes?"

"Are you Senior Constable Waldroup?"

"The nameplate on the door isn't lying. Who are you?"

"I'm Addy Zhuang." Zabel, who had been standing behind me, stepped around me and walked into the room. "This is Zabel Carvalho."

I could have sworn I saw him flinch. In an instant, his posture stiffened and his face turned impassive.

"I'm the Sherlock Holmes expert from the bank," I explained. "I'm here in response to your letter."

It seemed as if Waldroup were making a few fast mental calculations while trying to maintain a poker face. "What letter?"

"Didn't you write me a letter a few days ago, asking us to come visit you in connection to the two missing Loch Ness Monster enthusiasts, the sunken Loch Ness Monster prop from *The Private Life of Sherlock Holmes*, and you needed me, a Sherlock Holmes expert, to come and help?"

"I don't have the slightest idea what you're talking about, Mr. Zhuang."

I pulled the letter out of my coat pocket and placed it on his desk. "Are you saying you didn't send this letter to me?"

Waldroup picked up the letter and stared at it for a few moments. I noticed that his eyes weren't moving, which gave me the impression that he was trying to figure out what to do with it rather than actually reading it. After an extended silence, I asked, "That is your signature on the bottom, isn't it?"

"Yes…" I noticed a couple of little droplets of sweat forming on his brow. Why was he so nervous? Why was he denying that he'd sent the letter? Or perhaps he really hadn't written it? If so, who had? As his face was growing steadily paler, I was sure that there was something else going on, but at the moment my thoughts on the reasons for his anxiety were pure speculation.

"Are you saying you didn't write this letter?" Zabel asked.

He handed it back to me, now with a couple of oily fingerprints stamped upon the corner. "Why would I ask you to come up here? Wouldn't it have been easier to ask you any questions I might have had over the phone or through email?"

After reflecting on his comments for a moment, I realized that he had a point. As much as I wanted to see Loch Ness, the journey from London to Inverness was a bit long for my tastes. The lower half of me was not nearly as flexible as it normally was, and while most of the time there are few things that provide me with more pleasure than a comfortable chair, at that moment I didn't feel like sitting down again for quite some time.

From the way Zabel's nose was twitching, I could tell that she wasn't convinced by Waldroup's denials. "If you didn't write this, do you have any idea who did?"

"No." Waldroup shifted to the offensive. "Is this some kind of joke? Or are you just trying to insert yourself into a police investigation? Did you mail this letter to yourself?"

"Absolutely not to all three of your questions." A bit of inspiration flashed through my mind, and I held the envelope in front of him with my right index finger tapping on the postmark. "We're from London. This was mailed right here from Inverness. I can provide witnesses to prove that we haven't left London in the last few days. We couldn't possibly have sent this to ourselves, and we don't know anybody who lives here."

Perhaps it was the logic of my argument, or maybe he could sense the honesty in my demeanor, but Waldroup seemed to soften towards me. "I suppose someone could be having a laugh at all of us. Who exactly are you again and what are you doing here?"

I explained my job to him, and he didn't make me repeat myself a couple of times like most people do when I explain what I do for a living. Zabel used a lot fewer words than I did, contenting herself with saying only, "I'm an independent true crime reporter."

"Well look, you two seem like nice people, but you seem to have been brought up here on a wild goose chase," Waldroup said. "I admit that there is an open missing persons' case at the moment, but there's no call for you to get involved. Feel free to stick around and see the sights, but I don't think we have any need for your Sherlock Holmes knowledge here."

"You're sure?"

"Absolutely. Go take a look at Loch Ness, but then you can go home and work on your videos on Florence Bravo."

Zabel's eyes narrowed a bit. "And you had no idea who we were before we introduced ourselves today?"

"No, I didn't. I'd never heard of you."

"Then how did you know that I'm currently in the middle of a series of YouTube videos on Florence Bravo, whose husband, Charles, was poisoned with antimony in 1876? I mentioned the project recently in one of my recent reports. If you don't know who I am, then you'd have no idea what the subject of my videos is."

This seemed to have a sharp effect on Waldroup, and he started spluttering and actually appeared to be sinking down under his desk. Zabel pressed on, saying, "You *do* know who we are. You're familiar with my work, that's how you know about the Bravo case. The letter says you're a fan of my videos. Clearly you've watched at least one of my recent ones lately. So if that detail in the letter is true, and since you've just been caught lying about your knowledge of us to our faces, I think that I'm justified in theorizing that you're also fibbing about writing the letter. Why you don't want to admit what you've done, I don't know, but I'd like to find out right now."

Waldroup gulped down the last of his can of cola, and sagged backwards into his chair. "You caught me."

"You admit that you wrote that letter?" Zabel asked.

"Yes, and at the time, I wrote it, I was totally sincere. But now things have changed, and…" He looked at us with pleading eyes. "Can you promise not to tell anybody that I asked you to come here? Please?"

CHAPTER TWO

The Missing Monster Hunterz

Often when I see somebody caught in a lie, an odd rush of triumph washes over me, and I bask in the excitement of watching the liar squirm in the light of exposure. This wasn't the case with Waldroup. If anything, I felt rather sorry for him. He eyes were making the same plaintive expression dogs make when they help themselves to food off your plate when you get up from the table for five seconds because you forgot the ketchup, and when you get back all but three of your chips are gone.

Before I could start talking, Waldroup started stammering, and I decided it was best not to interrupt him, as I didn't want to stop him if he were about to say something interesting. The unintelligible gibbering continued for the better part of a minute, until Zabel finally lost patience, leaned over his desk, placed her hands on his shoulders, and started shaking him vigorously until he regained the power of intelligible speech.

"Sorry. Sorry." Waldroup pushed back in his chair, and held up a hand, presumably to tell Zabel to stop. She did, though from the look on her face, it seemed as if she'd get right back to shaking him if he didn't start answering her questions.

"Can you talk?" she asked.

"Yes. You deserve an explanation." After a long pause, Zabel started to lean forward again, which was enough to convince Waldroup to break his silence.

"You know, you could be charged for putting your hands on an officer." His backbone seemed to have grown back a bit.

"I'll produce that letter as evidence at my trial."

Judging by the rate that the blood drained from Waldroup's face that was check and mate. "Please don't show that letter to anybody. It would destroy my job."

"Well, we don't want that to happen," I assured him. From the look on Zabel's face, she would have been perfectly fine with seeing some negative repercussions to his career, but she didn't speak out and contradict me. "Why don't you start by explaining why you sent the letter?"

Waldroup gulped. "Everything in the letter was true. Those two fellows really did disappear a little while ago, and they were talking about searching Loch Ness for that big prop from the movie. When I wrote that letter to you, I really did want your help. I thought you might know something Sherlock-Holmes-related that might help us with our search. It was a shot in the dark, but I figured if anybody might know something connected to that *Private Life* film that might help us figure out where they might have gone and why, it would be you."

"I see. But what about what you were telling us earlier? Why didn't you just talk to me over the phone or video chat, and save us the trip?"

After a couple of deep breaths, Waldroup replied, "It's because I really wanted to meet you. Mostly Zabel, actually."

Zabel folded her arms. "You know Addy and I are dating, don't you?"

"Oh yes, I knew that. I've got a girlfriend myself, actually. I'm not looking for a new relationship. What I want is a more exciting side career. And I kind of thought that I'd be rather good at what you do. True crime. I thought I could start hosting a true crime podcast, mirroring your channel, and I hoped to pick your brain for advice while you were up here. That's the kind of conversation that works best face to face, don't you know?"

"So you summoned us because you want to be a podcaster?"

"Not just that. I thought you might help us find the missing men, too." He dabbed at his forehead with a paper napkin.

"Go on."

"No! Please, not here. Someone might walk in, and I could get fired. I'm begging you. Can we please, please, please talk about this elsewhere?"

Zabel and I locked eyes for a couple of moments, and then she nodded about one thirty-second of an inch. I agreed. Waldroup was clearly working on frayed nerves, and if we pushed him too far, he might crumble completely. "All right. When and where do you want to meet?"

He sighed. "I'll be off duty in forty-five minutes. It doesn't matter where we meet, as long as there aren't many people there. Do you have any suggestions?"

"Of course not," Zabel rolled her eyes. "We're new here. I haven't got a clue what's here and what isn't and what's open this time of evening and how many people will be at a certain place at any time."

"But we're staying at The Maroon Unicorn," I suggested. "It's a small inn, only six guest rooms, and from the pictures of their restaurant it's only got a handful of tables."

Waldroup beamed. "The Maroon Unicorn is perfect. No one I know has gone there in six months."

"Why?" I asked. "Is the food unpalatable?"

"No, it's actually pretty tasty, but the waiter's horrible. Rude as hell. Ruins the entire experience, but he's a relative of the owner or he's dating the owner or something. I don't know. I've never cared to have a conversation with the fellow. Anyway, that should be safe enough. We'll eat dinner there."

"Didn't you just have a hamburger?" Zabel asked.

"I have a fast metabolism. That was just a snack. I'll meet you there in forty-five– no, make that fifty minutes. I need time to change."

"Fine. We'll meet you in the restaurant then." Zabel didn't bother to say goodbye. She was out the door in four strides, and I hurried right behind her. When we were back in the car, I asked her what she thought of our new acquaintance, and she replied, "I don't trust him, but I don't think he's shady or anything sinister. I mean, look at him. He looks like he's a nervous wreck. I don't know if it's this case that's getting to him or if there's something else going on in his personal life, but the way he was twitching, he's probably had twelve cups of coffee so far today. Look at his eyes, he's not sleeping, so he's turning to caffeine."

"I agree he's got the caffeine jitters, but from soda, not coffee. I counted at least eight cans in the little recycling bin next to his desk, and those were just the ones I could see."

"Well, there you are, then." Zabel turned right, and I saw the sign for The Maroon Unicorn swaying in the breeze. "This place looks all right. The building looks pretty new. Hopefully that means reliable plumbing. I've had a lot of bad experiences staying at quaint village inns where all the guests have to share a loo the size of a breadbox, and twice I've found an unsanitary-looking chamber pot under my bed."

"I saw pictures of the rooms on the website. The toilets appear to live up to the highest expectations of the twenty-first century."

Relief washed over Zabel's face. "That's great to hear. I was having traumatic flashbacks to the time I went to Cornwall to interview a woman who'd worked in a nightclub run by the Kray twins. That night, I seriously considered keying a police car or something like that and getting thrown in jail for the night, because the cell in the police station would almost certainly have been more comfortable than my room at the only inn I could afford. Come to think of it, the breakfast provided at the prison would almost certainly have been tastier than the complementary morning meal provided by the hotel. One piece of cold, charred toast and a tiny green banana too tough to peel. I've never been in a room with spoiled wallpaper before."

"Spoiled wallpaper? I didn't know wallpaper came with an expiration date."

"Well apparently, back in the day, it was common for people to make a paste out of flour and water and use it to glue paper to the wall. However, the wet flour tended to attract mould spores, so over the years, as the patterns on the wallpaper faded, a huge colony of black mould would be growing out of sight of the hotel guest, but not out of smell. Not pleasant at all. Plus, I woke up at two a.m. and found a plump little grey mouse on the pillow four inches from my face."

"I think my imagination has come up with a pretty accurate mental image of how you responded to that."

"I spent the rest of the night in my car. When I got home, I had to get my suitcase steam cleaned to get rid of the odor. At least the interview was worth it. You know, that was my first video to pass a hundred thousand views?"

"I remember you telling me that. Good for you."

We made our way inside The Maroon Unicorn. I can't say I cared much for the décor. It looked like the living room of a seventy-year-old woman who shared a flat with at least a dozen cats. The room was liberally decorated with the kind of tchotchkes people donate to the church jumble sale and nobody ever buys. Upon reflection, that was probably how The Maroon Unicorn got its adornments.

The desk clerk was a tiny woman with a bun of white hair and a fuzzy emerald-green sweater. She was laser-focused on her crossword, and it took sixteen increasingly forceful rings of the little bell before she looked up at us.

"Yes, dears? Do you have a reservation for a room?"

"Two rooms, actually," I replied. "One for Zhuang, one for Carvalho."

"Hmm. Can you spell that?"

The Maroon Unicorn only had six rooms. I didn't think that it ought to have taken very long to find our card in the little box she had in front of her, but after spelling "Z-H-U-A–N–G" seven times, she finally located her record of my reservation, and Zabel, not wanting to join in on the spelling bee, reached into the box and extracted the card with her name in less than two seconds. The lady at the desk seemed not to notice Zabel's assistance, and after staring at the card for a few moments, she turned it upside-down and stared at it for the better part of a minute, moving her lips as she tried to read it, then realized she had it right-side-up the first time. She scratched a couple of bizarre hieroglyphics into the ledger in front of her with a pencil, and then pushed the registry book in front of us and asked us to sign.

Zabel went first, but soon realized that the pen she was offered had no ink. The second and third writing implements were similarly ineffectual, and Zabel might have had some choice words to say if I hadn't fished a working pen out of my coat pocket and handed it to her. It took the desk clerk a long time to find our room keys, but fortunately she managed to get them in our hands before our hair turned as grey as hers. After a moment's hesitation, we figured that she wasn't going to ring for a bellhop to help us with our luggage, and in any event I didn't want to waste any more of my life waiting for her to locate the desk bell.

I took three of Zabel's bags in addition to my own–she had brought five pieces of luggage to my one. It took a bit of strategic balancing, but I managed to tuck the two smaller cases under my arms and pick up the larger two with my hands. We made our way up the narrow staircase. Zabel's room looked pretty comfortable, though the heavy emphasis on unicorn-themed artwork made the room fall just shy of tasteful. I left her bags in a corner, and we agreed to meet in the restaurant in twenty minutes.

My own room was at the opposite end of the corridor, and I was pleased to see that it was distinctly lighter on the unicorns than Zabel's quarters, though the interior decorator had gone all-out on the other part of the establishment's name, and the room's furnishings were nearly monochromatic thanks to an overabundance of maroon. While Zabel's room was filled with artwork of mythical horned beasts, my room's walls were largely filled with massive bookcases, filled with tomes that were pretty much all older than I was.

After a bit of unpacking and a quick wash, I made my way downstairs and selected a table in the corner of the restaurant. It was a pleasant-looking dining room, but much like the overabundance of unicorns, the interior decorating made me feel uncomfortable. The walls were lined with china plates, painted with all sorts of pastoral scenes and animals with preternaturally large eyes. Each was held to the wall by a pair of tiny tacks, with each fragile-looking plate resting precariously upon them, with nothing else securing the flatware. They gave the sense that if I talked too loudly, the vibrations from my voice would send every last plate crashing to the rather unyielding carpet. It made me wonder if the plates were insured for triple their value, or perhaps The Maroon Unicorn's business plan was based on their charging guests with a strict "You break it, you bought it" policy.

As the waiter handed me a menu, I could immediately see what Waldroup had been talking about earlier. Never before had a member of the food service industry been able to convey just how much contemptuous disdain he held me in with a wordless twitch of his nose. When I thanked him for the menu, he looked at me in the same manner I expect that members of the Royal Family respond with when people ask them about their portrayals on *The Crown*.

Zabel arrived a minute later, having changed into a dark blue jumper and long grey skirt. I had a brief moment of unease, wondering if she had expected me to smarten up my wardrobe for dinner, but the smile she gave me reassured me that I was still meeting her admittedly high standards as a boyfriend.

I rose and pulled Zabel's chair out for her, and shortly after she'd settled herself next to me, the waiter sidled up to our table asked, "Would you like to see the wine menu?"

"No thank you," Zabel replied.

"We're not really drinkers," I explained.

The waiter gave us a look like we were something he'd left in his handkerchief, and snapped, "Our food is best appreciated when paired with an appropriate wine!"

"How good can the food be if you have to be half-sloshed to appreciate it?" I wondered, not realizing that I'd said it both aloud and far more audibly than I ought to have. From the look on the waiter's face, I no longer felt comfortable with him having access to anything we were going to eat.

Zabel started to put a hand over her mouth in order to cover her chuckle, but lowered it once she decided she didn't care if our waiter saw her laughing or not.

It's possible that our waiter might have had a cutting retort for us, but before he could reply, Waldroup sauntered into the dining room. He had changed out of his policeman's uniform, and was now wearing a scuffed bomber jacket and jeans with small holes in the knees. He also was wearing a baseball cap and sunglasses indoors, apparently under the mistaken impression that they served as an impenetrable disguise, and that wearing sunglasses and a hat indoors would not draw the slightest amount of attention.

As Waldroup joined our table, the waiter slapped three menus down, and snapped to him, "I don't know if you realize this, *sir*, but your dungarees are in a state of disrepair. And hats are not allowed inside the dining room." Our waiter flicked his thumb and forefinger against the bridge of Waldroup's cap, sending it fluttering down to the tabletop.

With a groan, Waldroup replied, "Ah, Abhorson. I see you're providing the same level of friendly service that we've all been accustomed to here."

The menus had been in our hands for only three seconds, but Abhorson queried, "Are you ready to order?"

I quickly scanned the menu, and realized that there wasn't much in the way of options. There was one appetizer, one entrée, and one dessert, and I didn't have the slightest clue of what any of it was. No descriptions, just words I'd never seen before that moment.

"I recommend ordering the full prix fixe three-course menu," Waldroup informed us. "It's a very good deal, and some of the best food in town."

"But what *is* it?" Zabel asked, and I must say, I was glad that she was as confused as I was.

"Three prix fixe dinners," Waldroup ordered, without bothering to confirm we wanted all of that food. As Abhorson stomped away, Waldroup explained, "Cullen skink– that's a haddock, potato, and onion soup. Scottish stovies and rumbledethumps– Scottish stovies is a meat stew traditionally made with whatever's left behind from the Sunday roast. The name's derived from what was cooked on the stove, you see. Rumbledethumps is a vegetable casserole topped with mashed potatoes. And cranachan is a pudding made from raspberry, whipped cream, and oats, maybe with a touch of whisky as well."

Personally, I have a deep-seated animus towards restaurants that take the attitude, "You'll eat what we serve you and like it." Growing up, I attended a school where the ladies who served our lunches embraced that ideology, and I find myself preferring establishments that offer the customers at least some sort of agency regarding their food, even if it's something as basic as, "You can put brown sauce on it or not– do whatever you want." There were no condiments on the table, not even salt and pepper, which warned me at once that this was the sort of eatery that had very set ideas about what their food should taste like, and the diners were expected to fall in line.

Zabel was all business. "So, we're here now and we're relatively alone. How about telling us exactly why you sent Addy that note and why you denied it?"

After making an odd-sounding gulp, Waldroup took the plunge and bared his soul. "Well, the fact of the matter is, I'm not very fond of my job, and truth to tell, I'm not very skilled at it, either. My father was a policeman, as was my grandfather. All of my brothers and uncles are policemen, though we all work in different towns. It's not really like I had much of a choice in the matter. One minute I was a carefree teenager at school, and the next thing I know I'm at the Training and Recruitment Centre, learning how to serve in law enforcement."

"I'm sorry you don't like your career." It was really a silly thing to say, but Waldroup looked so dejected I felt like I had to offer some basic gesture of sympathy.

"Thank you. I shouldn't say I'm totally inept at the job. It's the detecting bit that I just don't have the knack for, you see. I'm rather like the detectives in a lot of fiction books, the ones who always need an amateur sleuth's help to solve the crime. Only I don't have any amateur sleuths to help me. You two are the first I've ever met. I've closed my share of cases, but easy ones, where the criminals were caught on CCTV and the like. There is one part of the job that I'm absolutely first-class at, actually. Paperwork. There's a lot of forms to handle, and I can fill them out like a champion."

"Your superiors must be so pleased with you."

If Waldroup detected the notes of sarcasm in Zabel's voice, he didn't show it. "I learned early on that if there's one thing the top brass appreciates, it's properly filled-out paperwork. But I'm in a bit of a jam now. Most of my superiors at the station and the best investigators are out, either on maternity leave or away at specialized training or dealing with various health issues. So when those two fellows disappeared, it fell upon me to find out what happened to them. Unfortunately, I've been treading water trying to find a proper clue, and frankly I'm stumped. I have no idea what happened to those two."

"Please start at the beginning," I said. "Who are these people, what are they doing here, and when did they disappear?"

"They call themselves "The Monster Hunterz. Val Slorrance and Fergie Gastrell. Have you heard of them? They spell "Hunterz" with a 'z' instead of an 's,' by the way."

Improper spelling chafes me in ways I can't explain. "Why do they do that? Don't they have spellcheck?"

"Apparently they started out spelling it normally, but then their legal team realized there's an American writer who uses the phrase in his books. There wasn't any official legal challenge, but they decided to head off any problems by switching to a zed. The spelling seems to suit their personal characters better, really."

"So who are they and how do they make their living?"

"They're YouTubers, like you." He gave a little nod to Zabel. "They're very well-funded, because they both come from wealthy families and have the kind of trust funds that make me want to cry when I compare them to my bank account. Actually, come to think of it, they get a lot of funding from sponsors. I don't know why companies would want to back their videos, but they do."

I smiled. "My friend Jasper's a YouTuber, too, focusing on entertainment. He gets all sorts of companies to back his videos, from shaving supplies to meal prep kits. It's funny, they send him the meal prep kits, with all the food packaged and portioned, but he can't be bothered to throw it all in a pan and stir it up himself. We have to make it for him."

"At least when we can get to the kit before he eats the little packets of shredded cheese or the chopped nuts first, so we have to make the enchiladas or whatever they send him with some of the ingredients missing or substituted," Zabel laughed. "Who funds the Monster Hunterz?"

"Um, I know they've been backed by an energy drink company, and I think that there's a men's magazine that supports them as well. And a something-or-other Maker, I forget. Basically, they go all over the world looking for famous monsters. They spent six months going all around American woodlands looking for Bigfoot, they were in the Himalayas for seven weeks, attempting to find the Yeti… They were just in Mexico looking for the Capybara, too."

"Do you mean 'Chupacabra?'" I asked. "The Chupacabra is a supposed Latin American monster who preys upon goats. The Capybara is a big South American rodent, and because it lives in water, four centuries ago, the Pope declared that it counted as fish and could be eaten during Lenten meatless days. This wasn't because he really believed it was a fish. It was because food was scarce and the Pope wanted the faithful to have sufficient protein and the fasting rules aren't meant to be punitive…" I was losing Waldroup. He was looking straight through me, and I knew it was time to cut the history lesson short. "So, the Loch Ness Monster was next on their list?"

"Yes, it was. Their plan was to–" Waldroup was interrupted when our waiter flounced in with a tray holding three soup bowls full of Cullen skink. Tucking his napkin into his belt, Waldroup told us, "They even put a poached egg on it. Lovely orange yolk, you can tell it's free range. Nice." Abhorson didn't respond to his show of appreciation. He turned up his nose and stomped back into the kitchen. They must have been paying him well, as he didn't seem to be the least bit desperate for gratuities.

"What do you think?" I asked Zabel after the first few spoonfuls.

"I admit, I was put off by a name that sounds like a minor Harry Potter villain, but this is actually rather tasty. Don't tell our waiter, though. I don't want to say anything that could potentially provide him with any level of satisfaction."

Agreeing, I said, "It's a nice fish chowder, very creamy. It's warm and soothing, pleasant seasoning. I also concede I was skeptical, but it's good."

"I knew you'd like it," Waldroup beamed. He seemed to take a considerable amount of pride in his local cuisine, and I decided that no matter what the quality of the upcoming courses, I would play up how much I was enjoying it in order to keep Waldroup happy and willing to keep talking. I was trying to convey my strategy to Zabel completely through my eyes. I have no idea if she picked up on my message.

Our waiter sidled up to our table, saying, "I trust your food is to your liking." It wasn't a hopeful statement. It was more of a veiled threat, as if to warn us that any complaints would be met with a swift and devastating response that would leave us chastened and humiliated. He also bared his teeth like a wolf as he spoke to us, which is not an expression I'd ever seen a waiter make before in full view of the diners.

We all mumbled our approval of the food, and Abhorson returned to the kitchen. Zabel's better at speaking wordlessly with her eyes than I am. One quick glimpse at her, and I knew that she was thinking, "If this soup wasn't so good, I'd toss it right into his face." I have no idea how effectively I managed to convey my agreement.

I decided it was time to move the conversation away from the Cullen skink. "So, the goal of the Monster Hunterz was…"

"Well, their stated goal is always to find indisputable evidence of the monster they're searching for, and as you might have guessed, they've never been successful. They have claimed to have found tufts of Bigfoot's fur in brambles, and they declared that they discovered the Yeti's footprints in the snow high on a mountain peak, and they did provide video evidence of both of them, but as you can imagine, I and about a thousand commenters had some thoughts about the genuineness of the fur and footprints. Anyway, they've built up quite a following online, but the thing is, their schtick is starting to run a little thin."

I nodded. "Sounds right to me. You can only hunt monsters for so long, and after a while, when you don't even come up with Elmo from *Sesame Street*, people start to lose interest."

"You've hit the nail on the head," Waldroup agreed. "From what I heard, they recently lost one of their biggest sponsors – a body spray company, I believe. So to get back on top of the YouTube algorithms, they decided they absolutely had to come up with something connected to the Loch Ness Monster."

"What were they going to do?" Zabel asked. "Cut out some plastic shards and call them scales? Paint an oblong rock and say it was Nessie's egg?"

"Well no… they were looking for the long-lost prop from the Billy Wilder movie. They were hoping to raise it up from the bottom of the loch, and I don't know if they were actually going to float it in the water and claim it was really Nessie, or if they were just going to play up finding a piece of Hollywood memorabilia, or what," Waldroup answered.

"Would they really go so far as to try to fake the Loch Ness Monster?" Zabel wondered. "After all, only a tiny fringe segment of the viewing public would tune into a

YouTube channel expecting a couple of guys to finally discover mythical creatures no one's ever seen before. Surely their viewers know that it's all just for show?"

"Have you watched their videos?"

"No."

"Well, you should. They've got a pretty good rapport. They're funny fellows, and even if they're up to their waists in snow or flat on their backs after slipping on mud in the forest, they're entertaining. They've got some nice banter, and they spend most of their time going on rambling tears about all sorts of topics. They don't really need to bop all around the world trying to catch monsters – they could do exactly what they're doing filming themselves on a sofa in a basement, but it wouldn't have the same cachet. Who wants to watch a show about two guys in a living room chatting? But put that same dialogue in an exotic location, supplemented with the hunt for a legendary creature, well then you've got a high-concept premise that will get viewers liking, sharing, and subscribing."

I looked at Waldroup for a couple of moments, mentally evaluating the enthusiasm in his voice. "You've really thought a lot about what makes internet videos catch on, haven't you?"

He squirmed for a bit and toyed with his spoon again, and then he rapidly took a few quick sips of his Cullen skink. Just as I thought he had decided to ignore my question, he finally spoke. "I told you, I don't really think policing is for me. I think I could be a pretty effective YouTuber if I got the chance. I've been doing a lot of research, watching the top channels and sizing up what makes them work. But I need a hook, and I'd really like to talk with someone successful. That's why I wrote to you. Zabel – may I call you Zabel? You've managed to carve out a pretty impressive niche for yourself."

"I make enough to pay my bills, but it's a house of cards. With the algorithms changing and new people casting their hats into the ring every week, you can't count on ad revenue and subscribers paying to see exclusive content on your private channels. I've no idea if I'll be able to make ends meet in a year from now."

"But why did you get into the business in the first place?"

"I had a journalism degree and no major outlet willing to hire me, and I had an interest in true crime reporting, so I decided to go for it, hoping that the BBC or some other network would see me and hire me. Unfortunately, lots of other wannabes had the same idea, and I've been left on my own. Honestly, you may not be thrilled with it, but I really think that you need to hang on to your law enforcement position. They'll always need people to solve crimes even if they don't have the jobs for crime reporters."

"But…"

Zabel decided she'd had enough talking about her career woes. "Enough about trying to break into the business. What about Val Slorrance and Fergie Gastrell? Do you know anything else about them?"

"I never met them myself, but based on everything I know so far, they were pretty well-liked fellows. Friendly, good-natured. I've heard that they were 'bit of a lad' types, but I've found no reports of any complaints or allegations against them. Their records are spotless, aside from three minor traffic and parking violations for Gastrell.

Their friends all love them, and even their ex-girlfriends – and they certainly do have a lot of former flames – speak warmly of them. If anybody wished them harm, I've found no evidence of a personal animus against either of them."

"So what happened?" I asked.

"A couple of weeks ago, Slorrance and Gastrell showed up at Loch Ness, setting up their plans for their latest film shoot. They introduced themselves to a lot of the locals and started interviewing them about their experiences with Nessie – had any of them ever seen the monster, and if so, when and where?"

Zabel scraped the last of her Cullen skink out of her bowl. "Did they talk to a lot of people?"

"Oh, yes. Several dozen, actually. Both locals and tourists. They recorded all of their conversations, and apparently an awful lot of people wanted to appear in a popular YouTube series. I talked to several of them, and most of them confessed right away that they made up all sorts of cock and bull stories about seeing Nessie's head in the moonlight, or leaving a tuna fish sandwich on a picnic table, and then stepping away briefly to buy a soda, and as they returned, they saw this enormous reptilian head darting out of the water and snatching the sandwich. One woman claimed to have been walking her little dog by the loch's edge, only to have the poor wee puppy eaten by the monster. All rot, as they were all happy to concede. No doggos have been harmed at Loch Ness, although one fellow really did lose his tuna sandwich there, but a large bird swooped down and snatched it up. Nessie wasn't the thief. As far as I can tell, the general consensus is that the pair were harmless self-promoters, and everybody seemed to think that it would all be in good fun to give their legs a good pull. Well, not much of a crime to lie to a YouTuber, is it?"

"Not as far as I know," Zabel replied. "And given the number of men who've claimed to be highly influential media magnates who could turn me into one of the biggest names in journalism if I go away somewhere with them for the weekend, it's pretty fortunate that lying to YouTubers isn't illegal, because if it were, the prisons would be full to bursting."

"Wait," I said. "How many–"

"Nothing happened with any of them, don't worry, Addy. I could smell their phoniness a mile off. But it's amazing how convinced they are that women will buy what they're selling. Maybe they've tried it before with other ambitious journalists and met with lots of success. I really don't want to know."

Striving mightily to hide my relief, I asked, "So then, what happened to the Monster Hunterz?"

"Not long before I sent you that letter, they just vanished. The night before they disappeared, they had few rounds of drinks at a local pub, taking a few more interviews with people who were lying about seeing Nessie." Waldroup was interrupted by our waiter's return, as he snatched up our bowls. Zabel's and mine were empty, but Waldroup's was still a quarter full. He managed to blurt out "I'm not–" but he didn't manage the "finished." Abhorson shot him such a piercing look that he decided the last few spoonfuls just weren't worth it. Waldroup seemed to be so chastened he was unable to speak for another thirty seconds, when Abhorson brought us our entrees with the level of warmth and graciousness to which we were beginning to become accustomed.

As soon as our waiter was safely back in the kitchen, we turned to our meals. "So this is Scottish stovies and rumbledethumps?" I asked. "I hope it's as much fun to eat as it is to say." The stew was indeed hearty and the meat was tender. Cabbage usually doesn't sit well with me, so I was a little less enthusiastic about the rumbledethumps, but the mashed potato topping was well-seasoned, and Zabel seemed to be enjoying hers.

"The bottom of my rumbledethumps is a bit burnt," Waldroup muttered.

"Mine's fine," Zabel replied. "Do you want to complain to the waiter?"

"No." Waldroup answered with firm decisiveness.

Respecting his decision, I asked, "So, going back to where you left off, the Monster Hunterz spent the evening drinking with locals at a pub?"

"That's right. After last orders, they said their goodbyes and went back to their hotel. We're not sure if they ever made it back or not. They left their car at the hotel, as the pub was only a minute's walk down the street. The bartender saw them leave, and didn't notice anybody following them. No one at the hotel saw them return, but no one was on desk duty that time of night, and all the other guests were in their rooms, so that doesn't prove anything. Maybe they made it back, maybe they didn't. The hotel staff first realized they were missing around lunchtime the next day, when a parcel was delivered to the hotel for them, and they weren't answering their phones. Around two, housekeeping let themselves into their rooms and did some tidying up, and they weren't there. They were supposed to have lunch with a local group who try to take photographs of Nessie, but after they didn't show, the leader of the group called their mobiles and then the hotel. The staff checked and saw that their car was still there, and the next day, after they'd missed more appointments and there were four more big parcels waiting for them at the front desk, the hotel staff decided to call the authorities."

"You said that their car was still there, but what about their other possessions? You wrote in your letter that their diving equipment was still in their room, but what about their clothes, their wallets, their mobiles, and their recording equipment?" I asked.

"The recording equipment was all in Slorrance's room. Their empty suitcases were also in their rooms, and the closets and dressers were filled with their clothes. We don't know the exact contents of their wardrobes, but we do know that the items they were wearing that night are missing. Their wallets and mobiles were not in the room, and we can't trace their mobiles. All calls go unanswered. Otherwise, Gastrell's room had the makeup they put on for their videos, along with his laptop and a portable gaming device."

"Anything else? Any books or magazines?" Zabel asked.

"No. I don't think they're big readers."

"Didn't you say in your letter that there were some notebooks with some comments on *The Private Life of Sherlock Holmes*?" I asked.

"That's right, I forgot. I would like you to take a look at those if you don't mind."

Zabel set down her fork. "I remember in the letter that you asked Addy to take a look at those journals."

"Yes, there's a lot of references to Sherlock Holmes characters and stories in those notes."

"No one in town or in the police force knows anything about Sherlock Holmes? "

"Not as far as I know."

"So it makes sense that you would seek out an expert. We talked earlier about why you asked us to come up here, you said you wanted to meet us in person, or rather me, to talk about your move to a true crime podcasting career. So you had a totally legitimate reason for asking us here. Then when we came up here, you denied all knowledge of us and the letter until you were caught in a lie. This doesn't make sense. Why were you so worried about losing a job you don't even like, anyway?"

Waldroup was very nervous again. "Excuse me, I need to step out for a moment and get some air."

"No, you don't. Answer the question." Zabel was trying to look as intimidating as possible, which admittedly wasn't very imposing, but Waldroup's forehead was starting to perspire, and it didn't look like he was feeling particularly courageous.

Something that had been sitting in the back of my mind returned to the forefront, and I pulled Waldroup's letter out of my pocket. "Zabel, take a look at the letter again. Particularly, the stationary."

"What about it?"

"Feel it. See how thick and heavy it is. It's got a visibly embossed watermark on it. This is really high-quality stationary. Expensive. It's even light green. But I saw the official police station paper on Waldroup's desk. It was plain white, with the station's name and address on a letterhead, and it was cheaper-looking, too. I held the letter up to the light. "The watermark's kind of a repeating diamond shape, but there's also a big cursive "H" stamped onto the paper, though you wouldn't really notice it unless you were looking for it. This isn't police station paper, and it's not your personal paper either. So whose is it? What does the "H" stand for? It's probably the initial of someone with plenty of money."

I'd never seen Waldroup at work investigating, but I hope that he was better at interviewing suspects than he was being questioned himself. After a few moments of stammering, he cracked. "It stands for "Hunniraube." This is the personal paper of Lord Hunniraube. He's a very prominent figure around here."

"So what are you doing with his notepaper?"

"I'm kind of… well, I'm dating…"

"You're dating Lord Hunniraube?" Zabel asked.

"What? No, not him! His daughter! Phyllida."

"And Lord Hunniraube doesn't approve," I deduced.

"Of course he doesn't," Zabel replied, not waiting for Waldroup to answer. "How many aristocrats flip out with joy at the prospect of their daughter marrying a policeman who wants to quit and become a podcaster?"

Waldroup recovered his powers of speech. "Phyllida's not just Lord Hunniraube's daughter. She's his only child. She wants to host the podcast with me, actually."

Somehow, I didn't think that last bit would make Lord Hunniraube any happier, but I held my tongue.

Zabel pressed on, making sure that all of the pieces fit. "So let me make sure I'm following you here. You are dating the daughter of one of the most powerful men in the area. He doesn't know about your relationship and you doubt that he'll be particularly enthusiastic about it if he does learn about it. You wrote to Addy–"

"Actually," I interrupted. "I'm not so sure he did write this letter. I know one can get in trouble these days for drawing conclusions like this, but when I first saw the note, I thought it looked more like a woman's handwriting than a man's. I didn't think too much of it at the time because I wasn't sure if "Pherson" was a man's name or a woman's. But there was something odd about one of the lines in the letter. Towards the end, it said, *"The local authorities have found some notes…"* See what I'm driving at here, Zabel. *"The local authorities."* If a member of the police force had written the letter, why didn't he say *"We've found some notes?"* I think Phyllida wrote this."

"I'm really not much of a letter writer," Waldroup explained. "I wanted to write to you and get you up here to meet you, but I wasn't quite sure what to say, so I spoke with Phyllida, and she wrote down everything for me – now Phyllida's a great letter writer. You know, every week she writes me these incredible love letters–"

"That's a detail you can safely skip right now," Zabel said. "Get back to Addy's letter."

"Right, right, right. So Phyllida wrote down the letter, I guess she phrased that sentence from her perspective instead of from mine, and she used her family stationary, and I signed it and put it in the post. It wasn't until a day or two ago that I remembered that she'd used that distinctive green paper. And then I started panicking."

"Not because you were afraid that your superiors would be upset that you called Addy in, or because you didn't want to offend your bosses with your podcasting dreams, no. You were afraid we'd start showing this letter around, and someone would see the stationary and put two and two together that you were in a relationship with Phyllida."

"Exactly."

"But why?" I asked. "Are you so afraid of the professional or social repercussions if Lord Hunniraube finds out about you two?"

"It's more about the physical consequences," gulped Waldroup. "You see… Lord Hunniraube is, well, for want of a better word… eccentric."

"Do you mean "eccentric even for a nobleman," or "bat guano, somebody find a straightjacket his size eccentric?" I wondered.

"Dangerous eccentric," Waldroup explained. "We're talking about a man who's made it his life's ambition to kill the Loch Ness Monster."

Abhorson approached our table to remove our plates, which were still pretty laded with food. "Not now!" Zabel and I blurted out simultaneously. It was rather more forceful a tone than either of us were used to using, but when someone drops a bit of information like the one Waldroup had, you tend to respond with plenty of emotion.

Our waiter was clearly not used to be spoken to like that, and he turned up his nose and stomped away with what I presume he hoped was all of his dignity.

"Why does he want to kill the Loch Ness Monster?"

In response to my question, Waldroup took another bite of rumbledethumps before sighing, "He blames Nessie for injuring him and eating his pet turtle when he was swimming in the loch thirteen years ago. Have you ever read the book *Moby Dick*?"

"Yes," I answered.

"No," Zabel replied, "but I know the basic plot."

"Well, it's like that. Just substitute Lord Hunniraube for 'Captain Ahab,' and the Loch Ness Monster,' for 'The White Whale,' and you've pretty much got it."

"And he believes Nessie assaulted him and killed his beloved turtle?"

"That's right. Thirteen years ago the Lord Hunniraube and his half-brother – the half-brother is the from the current Lord Hunniraube's late mother's first marriage. The scandal about the dissolution of the late Lady Hunniraube's first marriage was a nine days' wonder of a scandal, but I shouldn't gossip."

"You're telling us how the man believes that the Loch Ness Monster is his arch-enemy," Zabel quipped. "The time for worrying about gossiping has passed."

"Fair enough. Anyway, one summer night the two of them had a bit too much drink, and then they went swimming in the loch along with Kendrew – that was the turtle's name – and by the time they got back to shore, Lord Hunniraube had a nasty wound to the head and Kendrew was gone. He's been blaming Nessie for the loss ever since."

Zabel and I found ourselves temporarily at a loss for words. "Wait…" I finally managed to say. "Are you telling us that Lord Hunniraube actually saw the Loch Ness Monster punch him out and swallow his turtle?"

"I don't think anybody knows for certain, really. According to one witness, Lord Hunniraube was about to jump off a rock with Kendrew for a cannonball, but it was slippery and he struck his head before falling in the water. No one else saw Nessie, but his half-brother pulled him out and brought him to shore, but he couldn't find Kendrew. When Lord Hunniraube came to, he kept insisting that the Loch Ness Monster had knocked him into the water and gobbled up his turtle. All I know is that he's one hundred percent convinced that Nessie is responsible, and I don't know how much is real and how much is imagination or drunken hallucination or what. According to village gossip, Lord H was always a bit loopy, but when he lost his turtle he went completely round the twist and fell into a bottomless pit of obsession. For all we know, Kendrew is living in some quiet corner of the loch, happy and unharmed. If you ever meet him, I recommend that you don't look directly into his eyes. They're like black holes of fanaticism and irrationality. I'm not exaggerating. If you look into his eyes, you're staring into the abyss, and it's nearly impossible to break away from his terrifying gaze."

We ate the last few bites of our meal in silence, and after our waiter, who was clearly trying to regain a level of control over our dining experience, removed our plates, I managed to ask, "Forgive me for asking, but is there a reason why Lord Hunniraube isn't… receiving more specialized care and attention?"

Waldroup wasn't offended. "I can understand why you might wonder, and Lord Hunniraube's lucid and competent about pretty much everything – enough to convince the authorities, apparently. He's also very skilled at – for want of a better word – bullying doctors into pronouncing him completely healthy in mind and body. In case you were wondering, I can assure you that Phyllida's perfectly sane, and she's the sweetest, loveliest woman in the world. Lord H's half-brother's got his head screwed on straight as well. Every family tree has an eccentric branch or two. As far as Lord H is concerned, he's a perfectly normal fellow with a few intense obsessions, particularly Nessie and voicing his dislike of anybody his daughter dates."

"So, you want to be with Phyllida, but you can't quite gather up the courage to be open to her father about your relationship." Zabel has little patience with men who are too timid to be open about whom they're dating because they're afraid of someone else's disapproval. She has the opposite problem with me. Ever since we first got together, she can't get me to shut up and stop telling everybody in sight that we're a couple.

"I'm in love, but I'm not foolhardy. If you'd seen Lord H's weapons collection, you'd know I have good reason to be nervous. He's purchased two of every deadly implement that it's technically legal to own in Scotland, all to help him in his hunt to kill Nessie."

"And His Lordship actively resists any attempts to provide him with professional help?" I asked.

"Yes, most recently six months ago. Ever since that fiasco, poor darling Phyllida's had to see a therapist herself three times a week."

Abhorson delivered three tall goblets filled with cranachan with a double portion of silent hostility on the side. Apparently their recipe was a bit different from what Waldroup was used to, because most of the white layers consisted of a soft cheese that Waldroup informed us was called "crowdie," with raspberries and oats between the layers. It was topped with a fluffy cloud of whipped cream, and fresh honey had been drizzled over it with a generous hand, and even more generous hand had poured the whisky. Waldroup didn't have to ask if we liked it. From the way we tucked into it, it was obvious.

"So, when do you want me to take a look at the Monster Hunterz' notebooks?" I inquired.

"Actually, they're at a laboratory right now. There were some odd spots and stains on them, and they're being tested to see if they're blood. You should be able to see them late tomorrow afternoon. In the meantime, would you like to meet Phyllida? She's running a conference at Hunniraube Manor this week. You'd like it, it's got a bunch of mystery writers there for a creative writing seminar."

"Does she often hold conferences at her family estate?"

"Oh, yes. Small ones, where the guests pay rather high fees to meet famous people. These writing conferences have proved very popular. She did a women in science fiction one last month, and a time-travel romance conference the month before that. It helps to being in a steady income, especially when her father's pouring every available penny into his hunt for the Loch Ness Monster. I'll talk to her tonight and get you signed up. No charge, of course."

Waldroup's mobile rang, and after a quick word of apology, he answered it. When he ended the call, his face was ashen.

"What's wrong?" Zabel asked. "Has there been news regarding the case?"

"Huh?"

"Was that about the Monster Hunterz?"

"No… it was my supervisor. Apparently, I've been suspended until further notice."

CHAPTER THREE
The Leading Writers of Their Time

That night I slept heavily. Perhaps it was the long drive that wore me out, probably the whisky in the cranachan played a role as well. In any case, Zabel nearly fractured her knuckles pounding on my door at nine in the morning, informing me I needed to hurry up and get dressed, because we had to attend the writing conference in an hour.

Ten minutes later I was washed, brushed, and clad in one of my favorite soft navy-blue jumpers and grey wool trousers. There couldn't have been that much whisky in the cranachan, as I wasn't the least bit hungover. Zabel was waiting for me in the hotel restaurant, wearing an emerald-green dress and matching blazer. There were a couple of other guests eating in other corners of the room. An elderly couple sat by the window, silently eating porridge. Zabel had spoken to them earlier, and apparently they had come to visit Loch Ness for their fiftieth anniversary. The other dining guest was apparently working on a dissertation on abnormal psychology and didn't want to be disturbed. A thirty-something woman in the other corner was poring over her notes, and I noticed she'd dribbled marmalade over several pieces of paper. She didn't need me to point that out though, as I heard her swear just barely loudly enough to be audible, and she dabbed it off with her napkin.

"That marmalade is very expensive. Please do not waste it." Our old pal Abhorson was apparently still striving to win the Employee of the Month Award.

As we waited for the waiter to take a brief break from chastising the other patrons, Zabel asked me, "Have you heard anything else from Waldroup yet?"

"I haven't had a chance to check my mobile yet today. Do you mind?" I always ask. My family has a very strict rule about no electronic devices at the table, but Zabel's a lot more relaxed about that. I still feel obligated to make sure. Running my fingers over the screen, I saw that Waldroup had texted me twice. The first two confirmed that his girlfriend Phyllida had granted us access to the writer's conference. The second stated that he would be meeting with his superior officer just before lunchtime in order to find out exactly why he'd been suspended. He claimed to have no idea why, but he suspected that Lord Hunniraube had found about him and Phyllida's relationship, and the volatile aristocrat must have used his influence in the community to get him disciplined for no good reason.

"I suppose that's the most likely explanation," Zabel commented. "After all, whoever's responsible for the Monster Hunterz–" she pronounced the "z" with as much derision as possible– "going missing wouldn't want him off the case because he was getting too close to the truth."

"Do you two often look at your electronic devices at mealtimes?" Abhorson sniped at us.

Zabel directed her most dazzling and insincere smile in his direction. "We simply had to do something to distract ourselves from our anticipation regarding waiting for you to bless us with your delightful presence. Ever since we finished our pudding last night, we couldn't wait for you to grace us with your serving skills again."

Abhorson glowered at her, with the unspoken implication that if there were snide remarks to be made in this dining room, he would be the one to make them.

Zabel ordered the tattie scones (which were potato-based breakfast rolls) and a pot of tea, and I, feeling like I wanted to try something I'd never had previously, did a quick Internet search that informed me that Finnan Haddie was smoked haddock and eggs, both poached in milk, with butteries, which were comparable to flat croissants.

After Abhorson left, I whispered, "If you ever give *me* a smile like the one you gave our waiter just now, I'll know I'm in trouble."

"Indeed you will be," Zabel replied, patting my hand.

The meal didn't disappoint, and once we were sufficiently fortified, we jumped into Zabel's car and made our way across town until we reached Hunniraube Manor. It wasn't what I expected. I had thought that this ancestral home would be some sort of ancient castle or imposing manor house. Later, I learned that the original manor had collapsed from dry rot a century previously, and its replacement had been rendered uninhabitable by a mould and a vermin problem, and it had needed to be torn down a decade earlier. Fortunately for the family, the insurance money had been sufficient to build a new structure, and Lord Hunniraube's half-brother, Lachlan, who was by all accounts a fairly shrewd businessman, had persuaded his sibling to refrain from trying to recreate the previous building, and instead to build a very modern conference center and hotel overlooking Loch Ness, which could be turned into a profitable enterprise.

The regular car park was full, so we had to travel a short distance down a back road, where there was a little row of spaces next to a shed painted brown with a green roof, probably to better blend in with the flora. The area was surrounded by a thick cluster of trees, and I couldn't see any other buildings from where we were parked.

As we stepped out of the car and made our way towards the building, a young, fair-haired woman in an apricot pantsuit approached us.

"Are you Addy Zhuang and Zabel Carvalho?"

"We are. Are you Lady Hunniraube?"

"Oh no, that title hasn't passed on to me yet, and anyway, I prefer it if you call me Phyllida. Philly to my friends, and you two can feel free to consider yourselves in that category." A serious expression passed over her face. "Have you heard anything from Droopy?"

I believe that as a rule of thumb, no good can come from being in a relationship where one partner gives the other a ridiculous nickname. That's why I am immensely relieved that Zabel has never seen fit to call me anything other than "Addy." Still, I don't expect everybody to hold fast to my personal rules, so if Waldroup was fine with this moniker, I wasn't going to pronounce the relationship doomed just yet.

"He says he's going to find out exactly why he was suspended in a few hours. He assumes that your father found about the two of you and has gone after Droo– Waldroup's career."

Philly looked stricken. "But that can't be. Daddy doesn't know about us."

"Are you absolutely certain?"

"Definitely! If he had, there's no way he wouldn't have confronted me. Whenever something's wrong, Daddy makes sure I know right away." The shadow of past traumas floated over her face. "Believe me, Daddy doesn't hide his anger. If he had reason to object to my dating life, he would definitely have thrown a tantrum."

Based on the tiny bit of second-hand knowledge I had about Lord Hunniraube, I was completely able to believe that he was a man of intense and violent passions.

Zabel wasn't interested in the star-crossed lovers. She was focused upon the missing Monster Hunterz, and asked Philly what she knew about them.

"Oh, *those* two. Quite a pair of characters. You know that they visited Daddy right before they disappeared?"

"Actually, no. We weren't aware of that."

"You know, normally people will go to extraordinary lengths to avoid listening to what Daddy has to say about the Loch Ness Monster. But those two? They were hanging onto every word he spoke!"

"What did your father say to them?" Zabel asked.

"I actually couldn't hear. The three of them talked in one of the conference rooms with the door closed. It was just off the main hall, so I could watch them through the large plate glass window while I was on duty at the front desk. I can always tell when Daddy's in the middle of one of his stories about hunting for Nessie, because he's always waving his arms around frantically, and he keeps jumping and shaking in his chair."

"Does he often get excited?" I wondered.

"He does when he's talking about finding and killing Nessie. That's his only interest these days – I can't even get him to take a break and watch the telly unless it's a documentary on the Loch Ness Monster, or possibly something on weaponry or big game hunting. It's been worse the last year and a half since my mother passed away."

"My condolences," was my reflexive response.

"Oh, it's all right. Mummy and Daddy hadn't been getting along for a long time, not since my father had his… accident. I think its effect on him had a devastating effect on her. The more obsessed he got with his monomania, the more strain it had on her. I never dreamed that she was in ill health until one day she collapsed, and she finally told me everything in the hospital. Mum and I never got along, but that doesn't mean that I wasn't crushed. I suppose I'm rather cross with her for keeping me in the dark, but I understand. She was a very proud woman, and the more I think about it, the more I realize she was intolerant of weakness. At least her own weakness. I suppose Daddy's condition really wore her down. Mental health is so important, but we don't talk about it enough. I think that my grandparents and some of my uncles…" She rambled about her family history of depression for quite some time before we were able to steer the conversation back towards the Loch Ness Monster.

A bit of unease flickered in Philly's eyes. "Is it all right if I provide you with some guidelines for dealing with Daddy?"

"By all means," I replied, a bit of unease stirring in my belly as I realized that guidelines were necessary, and I didn't believe that they'd be anything close to the protocols you were told you had to follow when speaking to a member of the Royal Family.

"Please, don't stare at him directly in the eyes for too long. Not that he minds that, but it tends to unnerve other people. The important thing is that you must never, ever look at the scar that runs down the left side of his face. That is crucial. That's from the wound that Nessie allegedly gave him that night. Don't suggest it was from hitting his head on a rock, please. If he catches your eyes looking there for more than a tenth of a second, there'll be the devil to pay. If you see a stain or a bit of food on his clothing, don't draw attention to it. Whatever you do, please don't contradict him or argue with him on anything, no matter what he says. If he gets your name wrong, just go with the flow, and I apologize on his behalf ahead of time. It's going to happen a lot. Also, don't comment on the cast on his left arm. He broke it two weeks ago when he climbed a tree in order to get a better view of the loch, and the branch broke, sending him straight to the ground. And most importantly of all, never, never, *ever* suggest that the Loch Ness Monster isn't real. I know it's a lot to ask, and I realize how ridiculous I sound, and I'm sure you don't want to have to cater to his… eccentricities, but please, try to remember, he's not a well man, and I'm truly trying to make the best of a difficult situation."

She took our nonplussed silence in agreement, and then suggested we go inside Hunniraube Manor. As we walked towards the main building Zabel whispered, "Why am I reminded of that scene in *The Silence of the Lambs* where Clarice Starling is led down to the asylum basement where she first meets Dr. Hannibal Lecter?"

I repressed a chuckle and hoped that Philly hadn't heard me. As there'd been no change in her pace or posture,

I'd hoped that the distance of twelve feet between us was enough to keep her from hearing. Plus, the wind in our faces was rather strong, so as I buttoned my long wool overcoat, I figured that the sound of the breeze had carried her words far behind us.

We rounded a corner, and Philly froze. "Oh! Daddy's here." She whirled around. "I forgot to mention something. If you were from Scotland, I wouldn't have to say anything, but seeing as how you're Londoners…"

The wind was sending Zabel's lengthy tresses all over the place, and as she struggled to restrain her hair inside an elastic, she asked, "What's wrong with being from London?"

"Nothing, really. Nothing at all. It's just that, well, people who aren't from Scotland tend to make jokes about his kilt. That's just one tiny step below denying the existence of Nessie. There's a medical reason for it, you know."

"So it's a prescription kilt?" Zabel quipped.

"No, no. Ever since he tried to draw out Nessie while water-skiing, and he let go at the wrong moment and crash-landed on a rocky area of the shore, he's had terrible sciatica. It's very challenging for him to lift up his legs to put on trousers, so he finds it easier to wear a kilt. You don't need to know this. All you have to do is not say anything about the kilt. Not even that you like the tartan. No matter what you say, he'll think Londoners are being sarcastic."

"Got it. Don't look in his eyes, don't look at the scar that was supposedly inflicted by a giant sea monster, and don't look at his kilt," Zabel replied. "How about his feet? Is it safe to look at them, or is he sensitive about his toenails?"

Philly blushed. "I know, it's a lot, and he's a very challenging man. It's just... it's not his fault he's the way he is, and I'm trying to protect him. Yes, he's... high-maintenance. But he's my father, and I love him, and I'm trying to help him. Please understand, I'm not trying to enable him. I'm just trying to keep him under a certain level of control. I know I can't always succeed, but just trying makes me feel like I'm doing my duty as a daughter."

"We understand," I informed her. "Zabel and I both put a high priority on family. And I think that I've been in a similar situation many times. My father is a proctologist, and I've had to run interference a lot when people feel compelled to tell proctology jokes. Actually, Dad loves telling proctology jokes himself – he's must know hundreds of them, and he's always telling them at social gatherings, like my brother's wedding. But he can't stand it when someone who isn't in the business tells those jokes. He thinks it's disrespectful. You can only make certain comments if you're in the brotherhood of proctologists, I suppose. I think he believes that only someone who has seen the things that he and his brethren have seen has the right to make light of their experiences."

"Oh!" Philly suddenly thought of something else that warranted a word of caution. "Don't tell him what your father does for a living. Besides the sciatica, he's got a lot of other... personal problems, and the slightest reference to a medical professional in certain fields will get him to go on long tangents about his health issues in certain regions that you won't want to hear. Ever since he's been diagnosed with hemorrhoids..." Her voice trailed away in the wind.

"Should we just pretend to be blind mutes?" By this point, Zabel was making no effort to keep her voice low.

"I'm sorry, I'm sorry. I just… he's been so touchy lately."

"What about his turtle?" I wondered. "Is that a sensitive subject?"

"Oh!" Philly's face flushed pink. "Thank you for thinking about that. That's very thoughtful of you. Yes, best not to mention turtles– or tortoises– or the name "Kendrew" either."

We'd journeyed down a little paved path, and as we went around a cluster of trees, I finally got a glimpse of a man who I assumed was Lord Hunniraube. He was holding a telescope to his eye with his right hand, and he slowly turned around when Philly called out "Daddy!"

He was a tall, powerfully built man. He was fifty at the most, possibly a few years younger. His curly hair was tousled from the wind, and it was half auburn and half steel grey, and his beard was two-thirds the first and one-third the latter. The hair on his shins was fully auburn. His arms appeared to be twice the size of an average man's. I permitted myself only the briefest of glimpses at his face, but I knew at once that his daughter was right, and that no good could come from staring too long at his eyes. They were, quite simply, the eyes of a fanatic. I had seen eyes like that several times before in my life, though never quite as intense. The only eyes that had come close to radiating that level of obsession had come my way a couple of months earlier, when I was trying to enjoy a doner kebab in peace on a park bench during my lunch break, and a militant vegan I'd never met before came storming up to me to criticize my dining choices. It didn't affect my diet, but from that day forth, I ate my lunch in the privacy of my office.

Not knowing where to look, I made a point of staring about five feet to Lord Hunniraube's left. Zabel and I both offered a polite greeting, and we received a curt grunt in return.

"Have my sardines arrived yet?" he barked at his daughter.

"Not as far as I know."

"They should be here by now." I felt his eyes turn towards us, and I forced myself not to meet his gaze. "D'you know why I've ordered fifty pounds of sardines? Take a guess."

Despite every instinct in my body telling me to keep my mouth shut, I found myself saying, "Does it have anything to do with trying to set a trap for the Loch Ness Monster?"

"Smart lad. Have you heard about the time a bunch of people got into a hot-air balloon and sailed over Loch Ness with a huge chunk of bacon dangling from a rope beneath it?" I had actually, and told him so. "Well, I'm using the same principle, only with a thin gauze bag filled with fifty pounds of sardines. I've already rented the hot-air balloon. They should deliver it next Thursday. I think those others erred by using bacon as their bait. Not that Nessie doesn't like a bit of red meat, but I think from experience and observation that marine life is more palatable to the creature. It stands to reason that a water beast's favorite food is more likely to be fish. Doesn't that make sense?"

What else could we say but "yes?"

His Lordship snorted. "I've no patience with those people who theorize that Nessie is descended from herbivore dinosaurs. It defies all reason. Now the theory that Nessie's related to the plesiosaurus, that's where I stand. They mostly ate mollusks, the paleontologists say, but there's reason to suspect they'd go after fish and small mammals if they could get them." He went on about the plesiosaurus for quite some time. His comments actually made me like him rather more. He reminded me of myself when I was six and could go for hours talking about dinosaurs.

I was hoping that I could use the topic of dinosaurs to segue into a discussion of Sir Arthur Conan Doyle and his connection to the Piltdown Man controversy, and possibly his book *The Lost World*, but it soon became apparent that Lord Hunniraube was only interested in talking when he was in control of the topic of conversation, as he waved his left hand at us with a dismissive expression. "Leave me. I need to return to my preparations." With that he turned around and put his telescope back up to his eye. Some vigorous hand gestures from Philly indicated that it was best to leave while the going was good. Zabel, usually persistent in her determination to get an interview with any potentially interesting subject, showed no interest in hanging around, so despite my own probably misguided curiosity, the three of us trudged back to the main building.

"If there's anything you feel compelled to say about him, don't hold back on my account," Philly said, resignation oozing out of every pore of her face. "I've heard it all before. Many times in fact. Perhaps that's one of the reasons why I'm so determined that my relationship with Droopy will work out well – men tend to worry that whatever Daddy has will pop up in me sooner or later, or possibly in any children I may have."

I really didn't know what to say. I am not a trained mental health professional, but I didn't see much chance of Lord Hunniraube being presented with the Most Level-Headed Aristocrat in Scotland award anytime soon.

Zabel was a bit more open with her opinions. "Are you quite certain that he's not a danger to himself or others?"

"The only creature on earth he wants to harm is the Loch Ness Monster."

"Perhaps, but what will happen if someone accidentally gets caught in the crossfire?"

Philly didn't have anything to say to that, and we walked in silence for another minute until we entered the main hall of the building.

The large quantity of weapons on the walls, presumably belonging to Lord Hunniraube, did not fill me with comfort. At least they weren't modern weapons, but if Sir William Wallace had accidentally misplaced all of his deadly objects, Lord Hunniraube could have provided him with enough pointy items to send King Edward I packing. I wasn't aware that so many antique claymore swords existed. There were at least two hundred of them on the walls, as well as a glass case filled with a little sign identifying them as "Andrew Ferrara" swords. Two glass cases filled with dirk daggers, mattucahlasses, and sgian-dubh knives were against a wall, next to a rack filled with tall Lochaber axes and Jedwart staves. I should point out that I didn't have any idea what any of these weapons were actually called before I walked into the hall. I simply read the little signs placed throughout the collection.

"This is the main hall," Philly explained.

"You should call it 'the armory,'" Zabel replied.

"Yes, Daddy has an intense interest in weapons. He's very concerned with finding the best tools for hunting Nessie."

"I doubt that a dagger with a four-inch blade will be of much use."

Philly nodded in agreement with Zabel. "He keeps the harpoons and other whaling weapons in the cellar. His strategy is to incapacitate Nessie, and then to attack close-up. He wants to look Nessie right in the eyes when he avenges Kendrew. Every day, he changes his mind on which sword or dagger or axe he wants to be holding when he finishes the job."

There was one large portion of the wall that wasn't filled with weapons. Directly above the fireplace was an oil painting of Lord Hunniraube. There was no grey in his hair or beard, so it must have been painted several years earlier. He appeared to be in his early thirties. Cradled lovingly in his lap was a small turtle, which I presumed was Kendrew.

Philly followed my gaze. "He had that painted three years before the incident. He never had a portrait made of himself with me or Mother." For the first time I heard some bitterness in her voice. I noticed that Kendrew had a distinctive marking along the middle of his shell. It looked very much like a Claymore sword.

I noticed that sadness was creeping into Philly's eyes as well. Before I could think of something comforting to say, she shook her shoulders and changed the topic. "Well, you're a mystery fan. Would you like to meet some of the leading writers of our time?"

"Sure!" I realized that I hadn't had the chance to see who was registered to speak at the conference yet.

"We don't have too many guests – just a couple of dozen. It allows for more one-on-one time with the authors. I try to give our celebrities a bit of a break during the day, but I stagger it out so that all of them have their own time to themselves every few hours, but there's always at least two authors on call to talk to the guests. The people signed up for the conference are mostly would-be writers themselves, looking for someone to give them guidance on improving their craft and getting published."

Zabel picked up a pamphlet from a table that remarkably was not laden with weapons. She gave a little gasp, following it with, "Pretty pricey for wannabe authors."

"Yes, I know our fees are high, but that's how we stay in business, and as long as there are people willing to pay these prices, I think we're justified in charging for them." For the first time, I was seeing that Philly wasn't just a dutiful daughter. She was a sensible businesswoman as well.

As this thought crossed my mind, I suddenly started to wonder if her father's condition might not be simply due to a mental condition. Could it be possible that Lord Hunniraube was faking or exaggerating his mindset? What if a chance at seeing the Loch Ness Monster wasn't enough to draw people to come for conferences? I'd heard about lots of large manor houses promoting the alleged ghosts that supposedly haunted the buildings. Supernatural tourism is very much a trend these days. Supposing Philly calculated that people wouldn't really believe in ghosts, but a "mad auld laird of the manor" could become a tourist draw himself? Anybody could believe in that. Was she using her father and his alleged backstory to attract people to her conferences? Was Lord Hunniraube actually an extremely talented method actor, and was he happily turning himself into a tourist attraction?

A little more thought, and I began to have doubts about the plausibility of this theory. First of all, even if Lord Hunniraube were the greatest unsung actor of his generation, I'd never seen any thespian able to replicate the level of pure intensity that I'd seen in his eyes. Truly, the Royal Shakespeare Company can only go so far when it comes to training people to replicate the gamut of human emotions. And in any case, the titled classes are notorious for being highly protective of their reputations. Would Lord Hunniraube really be fine with allowing the world to think of him as a man obsessed with killing the Loch Ness Monster? It didn't seem particularly likely to me. As a further point, would guests sleep peacefully sharing a building with a man who fills his home with pointy objects? It wouldn't take much to make people think of *Psycho* after seeing all of the knives on display, and pretty soon no one would want to use the shower during their stay.

Snapping me out of my musings, Philly said, "Let's take a look around to see if there's anybody I can introduce you to now. Why don't we take a look at the library?"

We went down the corridor and turned right into a book-lined room. A tall, tanned man was sprawled out on a couch, with a cowboy hat on the table next to him. He appeared to be playing a game on his phone, but the moment he saw us he stood, picked up his hat, and doffed it as he gave a little bow. "Miss Philly!" He had a deep Texan drawl. "Lovely to see you. And who's with you today?"

Philly introduced us to him and explained our professions. "This is Stetson McLennan."

"Author of the Ted Testosterone thrillers." He shook our hands with more vigor than anybody else I'd ever met.

"Ted Testosterone?" To be fair, Zabel's reaction was rather like how most women would respond when they learn about an action franchise that was clearly created entirely by guys, for guys.

"That's right." Stetson obviously saw the expression on Zabel's face, but he didn't take offense to it. I expected that he was used to it. He turned to me. "I suspect that you're familiar with my work."

"I am. My father and brother and I saw the movie adaptation of *Bombs That Go Boom* a year ago."

"What did you think of it?"

Fully aware that I was looking sheepish with Zabel looking at me with mild amusement under highly arched eyebrows, I decided to be totally honest in my review. "I really enjoyed it. The movie really knew how to keep the audience entertained with non-stop action. The fight scenes were incredible, and the characterization of the villains was terrific." I gave Zabel a smile that was meant to say wordlessly, "Look, I enjoy watching Jane Austen adaptations with you, but sometimes I need a movie filled with car chases and flying bullets."

"Glad you liked it!" Stetson gave me a slap on the back that was sufficiently firm to make me cough. "I insisted on writing the screenplay myself. I started writing because I was tired of never seeing the kind of movies I like, and I figured it was smarter to write them in book form first. My policy is that action needs to be consistent – if the audience is so anxious over the safety of the character that they're holding their breath, then they'll never be able to yawn. And believe me, if you give viewers the chance to yawn, they will. These days, moviegoers will use any excuse to check their phones during a movie. You've got to give them something they don't want to miss."

"That scene where Ted has to defuse four bombs at once, using both hands and both feet, all while being suspended from a bungee cord that was on fire, was great."

"Yes, that was one of my favorite scenes to write." Stetson's stomach growled. "Oh, I beg your pardon. The continental breakfast was tasty, but I'm afraid it was a bit skimpier than I'm used to back in Texas."

"What did you have?" I asked.

"Morning rolls with butter," he answered. "And tea. Pleasant, definitely. But I need some protein to set me up for the day."

"I'm dreadfully sorry about that," Philly said. "We were supposed to have some sausage patties to go inside the morning buns, but unfortunately, the cooking staff left the side door open, and the dog got inside, and he ate all the sausage. So we had to make do with just butter."

"No matter," Stetson replied with an easy air of graciousness. But if you'll excuse me…" He reached into his pocket and pulled out a yellow plastic packet with a little picture of some sort of cartoon creature wearing a red cap on it. "Buc-ee's Ghost Pepper Beef Jerky. I never go anywhere without it. Not just Ghost Pepper. I keep a lot of different flavors handy. But Ghost Pepper's my favorite. I love spicy food." He opened the bag, but before helping himself he offered some to us. Philly politely declined, but

Zabel and I both accepted. As we helped ourselves, he warned us, "It's got a real burn to it, so watch out."

Moments later, we both rushed for a large carafe of water that was on a corner table. I liked the jerky, but our tongues were on fire.

"I hope you two are O.K. You do get used to it. Can I get you anything else? A little milk might cut the burning sensation."

I was touched by Stetson's concern. Two glasses of water later, I managed to gasp, "I'm fine." A moment later that flames returned to my mouth, and Zabel and I both agreed that perhaps some milk would be a good idea.

"I'll be right back with the milk," Stetson said, but Philly stepped in front of him as he strode towards the door.

"You've got that page-to-screen seminar in five– actually, three minutes. You head to Conference Room Three. I'll make sure Zabel and Addy get their milk."

After a few more words of concern, Stetson left for his seminar, and the three of us hurried along the corridor and down a flight of stairs to the kitchen. There were two cooks arranging platters of sliced cold meat and cheese, along with plates of assorted vegetables and some loaves of sliced bread. They gave her slight wordless nods before returning to their work. Philly reciprocated with an equally subtle gesture, and led us to a large refrigerator. Moments later we were downing large glasses of milk and feeling more comfortable.

"Will you be staying for lunch? We'll have plenty at the sandwich buffet."

It didn't look like the most exciting meal, but at least we wouldn't have a supercilious waiter. At least as far as I knew. It was certainly possible that Abhorson had a second job, or even a brother with less talent for promoting customer satisfaction.

"There's something I want to tell you about…" Philly lowered her voice to a whisper. "Droopy. Let's go outside." A gesture towards the cooks informed us that she was afraid that they might overhear us. We followed through the door leading outside, and turned a corner into a little courtyard. Just as Philly started speaking again, she silenced herself when she noticed someone else standing there.

He was wearing a rather flashy suit and was smoking an e-cigarette. "Mr. Ginnungagap! Smoking is not allowed on the premises!"

"E-cigarettes don't count."

"They do on my property."

After a bit more quarrelling, the smoker extinguished his device and pocketed it with a roll of his eyes and a couple of vulgar words that were derogatory towards women under his breath, before storming away.

"Who was that?" Zabel asked.

"Gavin Ginnungagap." I explained. "I don't think that his real name, but he adopted it – "Ginnungagap" is a Norse term for an endless void at the beginning of creation. Apparently it reflects his personal beliefs on life and the cosmos; I read that in an interview in a mystery magazine."

"Are you familiar with his work?" Philly asked.

"I read the first forty pages of one of his novels."

"And you couldn't make it any further?" Zabel guessed.

"Exactly." Apologetically, I turned to Philly. "I don't mean to speak ill of one of your guests."

"That's quite all right. I don't like his work either. But he's very popular and people will pay to learn from him."

Zabel shuddered. "He looks like a real creep."

He certainly did. His suit may have been in dubious taste, but stylistic issues aside, it didn't really match his personality at all. Some people only look correct in a certain kind of clothing. The actor Charles Dance, for example, is the sort of man who looks like he belongs in a three-piece suit (or at least the Westeros equivalent of one). He'd just look *wrong* somehow in ripped jeans and a shabby hoodie. Well, Gavin Ginnungagap didn't look right in a suit. It was rather as if he were trying to bestow a level of respectability upon himself through his clothes, a sort of propriety that he simply didn't possess. It's not the sort of thing that one can say in another's person's presence with any semblance of politeness, but he had the sort of face that if you took one look at it, you'd feel at once that Gavin shouldn't be allowed to be alone with children under any circumstances.

What sort of clothing would fit Gavin's personality? If I were to allow myself to be frank to the point of potentially getting sued for slander, I would say that the item of clothing that one might expect to be Gavin's signature style would be a filthy trench coat with nothing underneath.

But Addy! I hear outraged readers saying, *aren't you being cruel and judgmental? Perhaps you've taken an unreasonable dislike towards his face, but you can't judge a book by its cover, can you? Don't you think that you should look at him with a little more charity?* To these people whose hearts may be well-meaning, I will reply that first, you obviously have not seen Gavin's face, and second, you definitely have not read any of his books.

"So exactly what kind of crime novels does he write?" Zabel asked.

"He writes erotic thrillers," Philly answered.

"I would use different words to describe them," I added. "Psychosexual noir novels. Dark, messed-up, dirty stuff. After I read the first couple of chapters of one, I felt the need to shower, and then spray my eyes and hands with bleach and disinfectant, and I seriously considered burning the clothes I was wearing when I read the book."

"They can't be that bad." From the expression on Philly's face and the use of the word "can't" rather than "aren't," I knew that she had never actually read one of his books, and challenged her on that point. With absolutely no pressure on my part, she immediately admitted that she was completely unfamiliar with his work, and that she'd only recruited him for the conference because she thought he'd be a draw, and his fees were quite reasonable compared to other authors.

"You know the premise of the book and television series *Dexter*, don't you, Zabel?"

"Yeah, it's about a serial killer who only kills other murderers."

"Well, Gavin was inspired by *Dexter*, and reworked it to suit his own twisted tastes. His major series is about a serial rapist who only assaults other rapists."

"Good grief."

"Plus there's lots of violent scenes that give the impression that he drew upon the *Saw* movies, but he thought they were too family-friendly."

Zabel shuddered. "I get the sense that something traumatized him in his formative years, and I'll be happy if I never know what that was." She turned to Philly. "You think Gavin qualifies as one of the "leading writers of our time" like the brochure says?"

Looking uncomfortable, Philly murmured, "Maybe I should start reading potential speakers' work in the future. I just don't have much spare time…"

"To be fair, he has a devoted fan base, even if I wonder about why they're so obsessed with his work. You should at least do a bit of Internet searching. Haven't you heard about his failed attempt to start writing for the telly?"

"I know he's been trying to turn his books into a television series for a while now."

"Well, that's not the most famous story. A couple of years ago, his agent managed to convince *Law & Order: Special Victims Unit* to allow him to submit a script to them. Portions of it leaked on the Internet recently. I don't know what they were expecting him to send, but it turned out to be a story about a New York City Central Park hansom cab driver who took an inappropriate interest in his horses. According to one news report, it was rejected before you could say "In the criminal justice system, sexually based offenses are considered especially heinous." Based on one rumour, and bear in mind, nothing's been confirmed, he was told not only that he needn't bother submitting another script, but that they'd appreciate it if he never watched their show ever again."

Zabel was quiet for a few moments. "I'm glad that we weren't properly introduced. He might have wanted to shake hands with us."

"Yes, we certainly dodged a bullet there."

A bit of chiming came from the pocket of Philly's blazer, and after a brief apology, she answered it. "Oh, dear. There seems to be a technology problem in one of the conference rooms. Will you excuse me, please?"

After the expected "of courses" from us, Philly hurried off, and Zabel and I decided to do a little more exploring around the grounds, though we chose not to get too close to the loch so as to avoid another meeting with Lord Hunniraube.

As we made our way along a large clump of trees, we discovered a carved stone sculpture – a turtle, or perhaps, judging by the size, a Galapagos tortoise. Clearly, they hadn't hired an interior decorator for the building and grounds. Lord Hunniraube had almost certainly picked out all of the artwork himself. I got a mental picture of his bedroom, with the bedsheets bearing a turtle pattern, and in-between the weapons on the walls were posters of turtles.

"Say, aren't you Zabel Carvalho?" A man in his late thirties, dressed all in black: turtleneck, jeans, boots, and leather jacket– ambled up to us. He had curly hair that matched his clothes, about five days' worth of beard, a thick Irish accent, and was eating a sandwich that must have been taken from the platters we'd seen being prepared earlier.

"I love your true crime videos." He shifted his sandwich from his right hand to his left and held his hand out for a shake. "I'm Cian Ícidhe."

We both recognized his name immediately. "We really like your work," Zabel informed him.

"My plays or my television work?"

"Both, actually." Cian had made his name in the theater as a parodist, sending up playwrights such as Harold Pinter in a not-especially threatening "comedy of menace" where the pauses grew ever-longer to the point of absurdity, and a thriller centered around the Shaffer twins with the same actor playing both Anthony and Peter. Zabel and I had seen a production of the latter about a month earlier.

It was his television show *Dame and Dibble* that was his biggest success. An affectionate send-up of both the gritty police dramas and the cozy countryside-set mysteries that dominate the airwaves, the series focused on the adventures of Brye Stoker, an incredibly tough police officer whose hard-nosed tactics and aggressive personality had earned him the derogatory nickname "Dibble" from criminals, civilians, and peers alike. After getting too rough with a guilty suspect who later had to be released, Stoker was removed from his position, but since he was too effective a detective to be fired, his superior officer had the bright idea of pairing him up with Dame Prudence Runcible, a sexagenarian aristocrat whose hobby consisted of solving the surprisingly bloodless murders that took place at the stately homes of her many friends and relatives.

The show played the "odd couple" dynamic up to the hilt, with the burly, tattooed copper and the bejeweled dowager teaming up to solve crimes like the heir to one of the most prominent families in England being found dead in the cellar of the headquarters of one of Peckham's most infamous street gangs, or a notorious human trafficker being buried under the dahlias in Lady Amaranth's conservatory. A trademark of the show was rapidly shifting the locales from the graffiti-scarred council housing of the most economically disadvantaged areas of London, to the palatial mansions that real-life members of the titled classes rent out as settings to film and television production companies so that the actual aristocrats can continue to afford to live there. At one moment, Stoker would be roughing up a drug dealer in the middle of a rubbish-filled alleyway, and a scene later, they'd cut to the Cotswolds with Dame Prudence having high tea, interviewing a suspect over blackberry scones and clotted cream. Despite my initial skepticism, it had become one of my favourite series.

Cian asked what I did for a living, and I explained.

He pointed towards a sundial on a carved stone turtle's back. "Didn't Sherlock Holmes have a pet turtle?"

"Only on the American series *Elementary*, with Jonny Lee Miller and Lucy Liu. There's no Clyde the tortoise in the original Canon."

We talked for a bit and walked around the garden. As we rounded yet another statue, this one made of granite, with Lord Hunniraube holding his turtle over his head in a pose reminiscent of *The Lion King*, we all jumped at the sound of frantic barking.

"That's the guard dog, Kratos," Cian explained, as he pointed to the Rottweiler in a chain-link fence pen. "He's quite the barker, but he quiets down quickly if you give him a treat." He walked about ten yards down to the pen, peeled a slice of ham from his meal and tossed it over the fence to the grateful canine.

A second later my mobile rang. "Hello? Yes, I see, Waldroup. Of course, we'll be there right away." After listening to his frantic worrying for another minute, I was able to convince him that we'd be at the police station as soon as possible.

"What does Waldroup want?' Zabel asks.

"He wants us to come to his aid. His superiors seem to think that he and the Monster Hunterz are involved in some sort of massive fraud, and somehow my vast knowledge of all things Sherlock Holmes-related can save him."

CHAPTER FOUR

The Police Have Questions

Chief Constable Griogair was smiling at us, but even though he'd been exceedingly warm and polite, I couldn't shake the feeling that he was waiting to drop the hammer on us.

"Thank you for coming on such short notice," Griogair said.

"Not a problem at all," Zabel replied. "Where's Waldroup – Senior Constable Waldroup?"

"Oh, he's talking with a few of our colleagues. He's not really in any trouble." Griogair spoke the last sentence so casually that I realized that I didn't believe him, especially considering Waldroup's anxious phone call. As I studied the chief constable's face, I noticed little red marks here and there, and I suspected that they were burst blood vessels – rather recent ones. Though I couldn't prove it, if I was a betting man I would've put a few pounds on my guess that Griogair had been doing some intense yelling lately, and I leaned towards the theory that the target of his ire was a certain senior constable of my acquaintance. He was in his mature years, but he was powerfully built and had the potential to be very intimidating if he were so inclined. I noticed a little chip in a keychain with the initials "GA" on it and the Serenity Prayer– it seemed as if Griogair was in Gamblers Anonymous, recovering from addiction– good for him. It seemed as if he were disposed to be friendly towards us, though. I noticed a photograph pinned to the wall behind him, with Griogair, Waldroup, and a few other officers standing around a cake saying WELCOME TO INVERNESS CHIEF CONSTABLE GRIOGAIR.

From the wall calendar in the background, it was taken about five months previously.

"By the way," Griogair said in that light tone that made me suspicious, "You needn't worry about hiding the fact that Waldroup has been harbouring career aspirations about podcasting or that he's in a secret relationship with Lord Hunniraube's daughter. We've been aware of that for a long time."

"Ah." I wondered if this was some sort of gambit to get us to confirm that bit of information. I doubted it – based on personal experience, I suspected that Waldroup would make eggshells look like reinforced concrete if a skilled police investigator started questioning him, he would crack so easily. I figured it was a fair assumption that he'd already spilled any and all beans in his possession. Still, on the off chance that Griogair was on a fishing exhibition, I decided that I didn't want to risk getting Waldroup in any more trouble if I could avoid it. I tried to convey my thoughts wordlessly to Zabel out of the corner of my eye, all while trying not to be too obvious about it in front of the chief constable.

"Is something the matter with your eye?" Griogair asked me.

Clearly I wasn't being as subtle as I'd hoped. "Speck of dust, I think." I blinked a few times. "All better."

"Good. Now the reason you're here isn't about our would-be true crime podcaster or clandestine relationships around the area, but because of your expertise with Sherlock Holmes." Griogair pulled a notebook with a blue plastic cover out of his desk drawer. It was marked with about a dozen yellow sticky notes, and he opened it to the first one. "This notebook belongs to the Monster Hunterz."

I should point out that he made no effort to pronounce the "z." "Most of it is pretty straightforward. Some drafts of dialogue for their videos. Nothing particularly interesting. But here..." he pointed. "Here's where all the talk about the Loch Ness Monster comes in, and they start talking about the sunken monster. We did a little Internet searching, but our computers are slow. Waldroup said something about it being connected to some sort of movie?"

"Yes." I started going into great detail about *The Private Life of Sherlock Holmes*. I thought it rather odd that he hadn't gotten what he needed from just waiting for a few minutes for the Wikipedia page of the movie to load, but as long as I could put my knowledge as a Sherlock Holmes expert to good use, I was going to run with it.

Once I'd paused to catch my breath, Griogair gave me a look that I chose to interpret as tolerant amusement. "All right, then. Now, all of these references to a "Lee" here. Is that a character in the Sherlock Holmes canon?"

"No, I think that's Christopher Lee. He plays Mycroft Holmes – Sherlock's older brother, a powerful government official. He has a small but pivotal part in the movie at Loch Ness."

"And these initials. Q.V."

"Ummm..." Two and a half seconds later I had it. "Queen Victoria. She makes a brief appearance as well."

"That's what I thought, but I wanted to get you to confirm it. Now moving along, they're talking about tying their next video to Sherlock Holmes as well. Take a look."

I read over the page, with Zabel leaning over so she could follow along with me. The handwriting was mostly in shaky caps, and from the scent emanating from some spots on the page that were clearly caused by dried liquid, I reasoned that whichever one of the Monster Hunterz had written this had been enjoying a stiff drink at the time.

The notes on the page read:

WEST COUNTRY (DEVON)

WE NEED TO ACTUALLY GET A MONSTER ON CAMERA OR WE'RE DOOMED

SHERLOCK HOLMES TIE-IN– CONNECT TO FAN COMMUNITY.

BERNESE MOUNTAIN?

GIANT SCHNAUZER?

CANE CORSO?

NEAPOLITAN MASTIFF?

FIND OUT WHERE HUNNIRAUBE GOT HIS

CHECK SHELTERS, DON'T WANT THIS TRACED TO US.

GLOW IN THE DARK PAINT?

CHECK ON P.M. – SOMETHING'S NOT RIGHT

"Can you make anything out of that?" Griogair asked me.

"Those are all dog breeds," Zabel noted.

"Yeah. Big, black dogs... Oh no. They wouldn't."

"Wouldn't what?" Griogair leaned forward with a look of interest.

I took a breath, hoping that my deductions were faulty. "I think that the Monster Hunterz were planning to pull a hoax about the Hound of the Baskervilles."

Griogair leaned back in his chair. "I know that's a Sherlock Holmes story but I never read it. Didn't see any of the movies, either."

"Well, it's set on the moors of Devon – Dartmoor, to be precise. The story has Holmes and Watson tracking down a supposed supernatural beast – a hound of hell that's been hunting members of the Baskerville family for generations. How much detail do you want me to go into with the book?"

"As little as possible."

"All right. Here's the Cliff's Notes of the Cliff's Notes of the Cliff's Notes of the Reader's Digest version. Do I need to warn about spoilers?"

"No. Just tell me."

"Well, it turns out there really is a gigantic black dog on the moors, but it's not a demonic creature. It's just an ordinary large canine that's been treated with something luminous and trained to be ferocious by the story's human villain. I can't be sure, but I think that once the Monster Hunterz raised the Loch Ness Monster prop, they planned to head to Dartmoor along with a big black dog. Not a vicious one. I bet they wanted a sweet and docile one that's easy to handle, and then they would make it up to look fierce. Then they'd play some howling, maybe plant something to look like something had been attacking people or animals, and then stage a big fight and capture scene with the dog. I don't think they'd try to hurt it or anything, just get a huge glowing dog on camera in order to convince the gullible that they'd finally found a real monster. And if anybody called them out on it, they could argue that it was an actual feral dog and deny planting it – although that wouldn't explain why it was glowing." I paused, having finished my theorizing.

"I guess that's the fraud Waldroup was referring to," Zabel remarked. "But why would you think he was involved."

"Waldroup's a good enough kid, but he's a trifle paranoid," Griogair replied. "Do you know who this "P.M." is?"

"Professor Moriarty? I'm not sure."

Griogair took a deep breath. "You know, Inspector Dankworth is an old friend of mine. He told me about you two."

"Really? How is he?" We'd made Inspector Dankworth's acquaintance several months earlier, when he'd investigated the bank robbery that first brought me and Zabel together.

"He's in good health, but his daughter's refusing to go to university or get a job, all so she can pursue a career as a TikTok influencer."

"Yes, he mentioned she had interests in that direction. And that he didn't approve."

"I'm afraid that his daughter's career may have a negative effect on his general well-being. His daughter's actually meeting with a lot of success on TikTok. And now it's having a negative effect on his own career."

A quick flash of alarm passed over Zabel's face. "Is she doing something…"

"No," Griogair reassured her. "Nothing scandalous. Well, actually, it is rather scandalous, but not in the way that you're thinking. She's calling herself 'The Copper's Daughter.' As you know, our mutual friend Dankworth has a bit of a temper, and over the years he's vented his spleen many a time about problems he's had with cases and habitual criminals. She's amassed quite a collection of anecdotes about him and his rants and temper tantrums at the dinner table, and now she's started filming little videos where she recounts these stories in twenty to thirty seconds each. She does a terrific job mimicking his voice, and she's started making a rather decent income from monetization. Unfortunately, it's made her poor father a bit of a laughingstock at work."

I didn't know Inspector Dankworth all that well, but I didn't think that he deserved to be publicly humiliated by his own kin. "That's not a very nice way for her to treat her father."

"No. Things are getting rather uncomfortable amongst the family, and his daughter says she wants to patch things up with him, but I suspect she's starting to run low on anecdotes and needs more."

We all laughed, but I stopped when I felt an indescribable sense of discomfort. I was starting to enjoy our conversation, but as affable as Griogair's eyes and tone were, I couldn't shake the sense that he was putting us at ease to test us. It certainly helped to know that my conscience was clear. But if he were trying to interrogate us without being too blatant about that point that meant that he suspected us of either doing something we shouldn't have or knowing something of use to him and withholding it, and neither case was a good position for us. It's hard enough to prove your innocent of an action and nearly impossible to prove you don't have a certain bit of knowledge in your head.

I tried to look over Zabel without drawing too much attention to the fact. I noticed that Zabel was sitting very straight in her chair, and she was squeezing her right knee, the top one when her legs were crossed. I knew that she was on her guard as well. Her posture was a dead giveaway to me, and I wondered if it was similarly noticeable to a veteran observer of human behavior like Griogair. And if he noticed that Zabel was on high alert, then how did Griogair interpret this? Would he consider her a guilty woman who was trying to protect her dark secrets, or would he come to the true conclusion, that she was an innocent person who knew she was under suspicion and resented it?

Griogair picked up his coffee mug and drained the remaining contents. "Well, the two of you have been very helpful and I appreciate it. Now if you'll please excuse my taking up a little more of your time, I'd like you to take a look at this letter. There's a fellow here in town who's blind– he makes his living doing whatever odd jobs he can manage with his disability. He dropped this letter off at the station shortly before you arrived here. He doesn't know who gave it to him, but as you can see… it's a bit eyebrow-raising."

He passed us a clear plastic envelope, and Zabel and I both held one side of the letter as we read it. It didn't take very long, given its brevity. It was printed in all caps, in Helvetica font approximately twenty-four point. The stationary was an ordinary sheet of white computer paper with no letterhead or noticeable markings. The message went straight to the point.

DEAR CHIEF CONSTABLE GRIOGAIR –

ADDY ZHUANG AND ZABEL CARVALHO KNOW MORE ABOUT THE MONSTER HUNTERZ THAN THEY'RE SAYING. QUESTION THEM, AND CHECK THE BOOT OF ZHUANG'S CAR. YOU'LL FIND SOMETHING INTERESTING THERE.

–A FRIEND

We returned the letter to the Chief Constable. "Do you want to hear our response to this piece of rubbish?" Zabel asked.

"If you are willing to share, then yes, please. By the way, I should tell you that you have every right to ask for a solicitor's advice."

"That's not necessary. We don't know anything about the Monster Hunterz. We never heard of them until Addy showed me the letter Senior Constable Waldroup sent us."

"I wasn't aware of their existence before that letter either," I added. "I didn't even know they spelled their name with a "z" until I was informed of this fact yesterday."

"So there's nothing else you can tell me about them?"

"Certainly not, Chief Constable."

"Now, I could get a warrant, but may I have your permission to search the boot of your car?"

"We have nothing to hide! You can–"

Zabel hates being interrupted, but I felt that the situation warranted it. "Wait just a moment. First of all, the person who wrote this note doesn't know very much about us. That's not my car, it's Zabel's."

"I was going to say that, but I got distracted," Zabel added.

"Secondly, if someone is asking you to search the car, then I think we have to consider the possibility that someone broke into the car and planted something – I don't know what it could be – in the boot. So if you open it up, you'll likely find something, possibly something incriminating, but we have no knowledge of it." I turned to Zabel. "Did you look in the boot of your car since we arrived yesterday evening?"

"No. Without our suitcases, there should be nothing in there except for a spare tyre in its own compartment, a little box of tools, and some garment bags with some of the clothes I change into when I need…" Zabel paused, not wanting to say that sometimes her work in crime journalism requires her to pretend to be someone else, which is why she brings along clothes that allow her to assume the identity of a maid, a nurse, a charwoman, or something like that. "When I need to freshen up a bit."

"And if you examine the car, I'd check for scratches to see if someone forced it open," I noted.

"I see. Now, you two strike me as very honest people, and I'm sure you want to be helpful. If someone planted something in your car, wouldn't you like to know what it is? And isn't it better if you allow us to look first, so we can examine anything that's in there?"

We considered this for a moment. "And if I refuse, you'll look into getting a warrant, won't you?" Zabel asked.

"Can you blame me for being a trifle curious?"

"I don't think an anonymous letter counts as probable cause," I noted.

"It's all a matter of opinion. The PF is a dear friend of mine, and as it's possible that these missing men's lives may be in danger, well, that might convince him that every possible avenue should be looked into, seeing as how we just don't know what the situation is here."

I didn't like it one bit, and I wanted to talk with Zabel privately, but she made up her own mind without any consultation with me. "I'll let you look inside, but I want to be there when you do."

"That's very understanding of you. Shall we all walk down together?"

As we left his office, I felt compelled to say something. I was worried that someone might have planted drugs or something else potentially embarrassing or illegal in the car. "If someone did plant something in the car, we need to insist they check our fingerprints," I whispered to Zabel. "That'll indicate that we didn't touch whatever was there."

Zabel nodded, but didn't say anything because the chief constable had slowed his pace and was now walking too close to us. I had an uneasy feeling that we were walking into a trap that would prove extremely difficult for us to extricate ourselves from, but I didn't see a way around it. If we denied him access, he'd become suspicious, and he'd probably send somebody to tail us, and how would we get the chance to check the boot first? Just when we thought we'd found a completely private, isolated spot to check it, the authorities would swoop down on us. If by some miracle we were able to borrow the use of a locked, windowless garage or something like that, and we found something, how would we dispose of it? We'd have to leave, and the police tracking us would see us tossing it into the loch or shoving it into a rubbish bin or something like that. I suddenly had the idea that Lord Hunniraube had somehow gotten ahold of a cache of illegal firearms in his hunt to kill the Loch Ness Monster, and someone, possibly Philly, had found them and tucked them into Zabel's car to get rid of them. In any case, we might just be postponing the inevitable, because a warrant could be issued at any moment, and the police could check out the boot find whatever was inside. *If* anything was inside.

As we walked out the main door and headed towards the car, I noticed that my mouth had gone dry. A uniformed police officer had joined us shortly before we left the building, and he hurried in front of us to inspect the boot. He bent down and pointed his torch at the car.

"Sir!"

"What is it, Constable?"

"There are some scratches and little dents here, sir. The paint's been chipped. I think they're right – someone's forced this open with a crowbar or some sort of burglary tool."

"Let me see!" Zabel appeared livid at the thought that someone had damaged her car, but Griogair placed a hand on her shoulder and held her back.

"If you please, Miss Carvalho. I think we'd better check this out ourselves. Please stand over there, with Mr. Zhuang." With that, he coaxed her key fob from her hand and stepped forward.

We waited about seven yards away from the car. Now I was sure that there was something that shouldn't be there, but at least, thanks to the scratches, we had a pretty solid defense that whatever item they might find had been planted there.

I realized that I hadn't taken a breath in some time, and I finally inhaled as the chief constable pressed the key fob, the car chirped, and the boot opened with a popping noise. From where we were positioned, we couldn't see anything with the policemen standing where they were.

The young constable gasped and jumped backwards. That wasn't a good sign.

Griogair stood there staring for a moment before turning towards us. "I'm afraid I'm going to have to ask you two to answer quite a few more questions."

Zabel darted forward past the young constable. Griogair started to warn her to stand back, but she was already able to look inside the boot. She whirled around and barely made it to a tree at the edge of the car park before she was violently ill.

As soon as I saw Zabel running off, I developed a new theory about what she'd seen, but frankly I was more concerned about her than confirming my suspicions. I rushed up to her, and once she was able to confirm that she was all right, I informed Griogair that I was going to get her something to drink, and I didn't wait for permission. I'd seen a vending machine on our way in, and a minute later I was back with Zabel's favourite diet ginger beer and a packet of mints.

She emptied the bottle in a few gulps and thanked me before emptying the packet and thrusting all of the mints into her mouth at once.

I didn't hear the chief constable walking up behind me. "Did you see what was in the boot of the car?"

"No, I didn't."

"But you're not in any hurry to find out what it is?"

"I have a theory. And I don't want you to be suspicious of me if I'm right."

Griogair took a couple of deep breaths. "I'd like to hear what you're thinking."

"It's simple. Zabel is not a particularly squeamish person. It would take something particularly unpleasant to cause her to become violently ill. We can rule out an illegal substance or a weapon, then. Therefore, whatever caused her to become sick had to have been something rather disgusting or grisly. Now it's possible that someone planted a dead animal as a sick joke, but judging by the seriousness of your face, I don't think it's something than can be written off as a mere prank. I'm going to guess that somebody placed a dead human body in Zabel's car." I sighed. "From your reaction, I know I'm right. Is it one of the Monster Hunterz? Is it Val Slorrance or Fergie Gastrell?"

He stood there, sizing me up, trying to determine if I were a murderer or if I was simply very skilled at deductive reasoning. "It's both of them, actually. I recognize their faces from the file."

"They can both fit in there?"

"They're both on the shorter side and skinny. They appear to be all folded up in the fetal position. It appears to have been a tight squeeze, but they're both inside the boot."

"Can you tell how they died?"

"No. I'm not a pathologist, and anyway there's no blood visible. However, the two of them are rock-hard and icy to the touch. I don't know if they were frozen to death or if they were killed and then placed in sub-zero temperatures, but I'm sure the investigation will clear up any questions."

Zabel was back on her feet, but the colour in her face still wasn't normal.

"Do you want another ginger beer?"

"Yes, please. And some more mints, too."

Once again I didn't ask for the chief constable's permission, but he felt compelled to grant it anyway. "Go ahead," he informed me after I'd already taken three steps.

When I returned with the requested items, Zabel gratefully accepted them and started drinking again, more slowly this time.

"I'm going to need to get a new car," she mumbled.

CHAPTER FIVE
Lunch and the Blame Game

I had expected to be thrown into a cell and given the third degree. Instead, Griogair patted me on the shoulder. "I'm pretty adept at reading people," he informed me, "and you and your girlfriend aren't murderers. You didn't know those bodies were there. So now, the question is, who put them there?"

"I don't know who, but I can give you a general timeline of when. We arrived in Inverness around six last night, and the car was parked outside in full view of everybody going by until we drove it to Lord Hunniraube's land. We parked in an isolated spot off to one side. We were there for just over an hour. If the bodies are still as frozen as you say, it's almost certain that they were placed in the car during that window of time."

From the expression on his face, I couldn't tell if the chief constable welcomed my suggestion or not. I was trying to be helpful, as well as attempting to regain some level of control over this situation. "We'll need to ask you some more questions," he informed me. "Will you two please come back inside?"

"Yes, of course. May we have a minute so Zabel can clear her head? That way, she can be as sharp as possible when she answers your questions. Plus, you don't want her to be sick again inside the building."

I didn't want to embarrass Zabel by saying that, but I needed to get a minute alone with her. "We'll just take a quick walk to the edge of the car park and back." After a few yards, I started to whisper an apology for the impression created by my words, but she cut me off before I could finish my first sentence.

"I understand why you said what you did. We need a moment to ourselves." She raised her voice as she said "I need a tissue." She pulled her mobile out of her purse, wrapped in a tissue. She leaned against me, positioning her arm so that the policemen couldn't see that she was rapidly texting. "He seems to be on our side," she whispered, "but we should still get in touch with legal counsel. Just to protect ourselves. So I'm texting Sanna."

"She's not a criminal lawyer, though. Don't you usually have a solicitor at your side when you're being questioned by the police?"

"Well, do you know any Scottish solicitors?"

"No. You do realize that even though Sanna's our friend, she doesn't work for free?"

"How much does she charge?"

"I've no idea. She does live with two flatmates and she doesn't own a car, so she can't be raking it in too heavily. Wait a moment. She's English. Can she practice in Scotland?"

In response, the mobile rang. A glance at the screen told us that it was Sanna.

"Hello, Sanna?"

"What the hell have you two gotten yourselves into? The first romantic getaway you've ever taken, and you wind up with two corpses in the car?"

We didn't have her on speaker, but even from twenty yards away the chief constable could hear her, and he hurried over to us. "Mister Zhuang, Miss Carvalho…"

"Who is that Scotsman?" Sanna bellowed.

"That's Chief Constable Griogair."

"Let me talk to him."

Zabel handed the chief constable her mobile, subtly setting the phone to speaker with a quick tap of her thumb. Griogair was clearly an observant man, however, and he made a great show of taking the phone off speaker mode before answering.

"Hello," he said. "Who is this?"

"Am I on speaker? Put me on speaker. I want to make sure all three of you can hear me." Sanna's voice was sufficiently strong for us to hear her even when the phone was set to normal mode.

I couldn't tell if Griogair was amused or annoyed, but he complied.

"Am I on speaker now?"

"Yes."

"Good. My name is Sanna Mahabir, and I am the legal representative for Adelbert Zhuang and Zabel Carvalho. I must inform you that you are not to question them until I can be there to supervise any interrogations."

"Miss Mahabir, I do not believe that your clients had anything to do with the deaths of those two men."

"With all due respect, I have no evidence to back up your statement. I don't want my dear friends spending even a minute in jail for a crime that they didn't commit. Are you planning to place them under arrest?"

"I already told you, Miss Mahabir, I do not believe that they killed those two men. I don't believe that Miss Carvalho had the time to text you this information –" he shot Zabel a look that I couldn't decipher – "but the two men found in the boot of her car were frozen solid. They haven't thawed a bit. That means they were taken out of whatever freezer they were stored in very recently, probably within the last couple of hours. It takes quite a long time for a human body to freeze solid. Several hours. The Monster Hunterz disappeared days ago, when your clients were in London. I just don't think they had the opportunity to kill them, freeze them till they were rock hard, and take them out and put them in the most incriminating place possible. And anyway, what would have been their motive?"

After a pause, Sanna answered, "It sounds like you're doing my job for me. You've put quite a bit of thought into their defense."

"They seem like nice people. I don't want them to suffer any inconvenience. Well, any more inconvenience than can be helped. We'll have to impound the car, of course, so our forensics team can look over it. So if you insist on being here, how soon can you arrive? You sound like you're from London."

"I'll have to check the train schedule and get back to you. I'll try to be there by evening. Will that be convenient?"

"I suppose it will have to be."

"Very good. I don't want my friends – clients – sitting around a police station all day. May I presume that they are free to go?"

Griogair thought about it for a few seconds. "Well, they don't have a vehicle anymore, so it's not like they'll be able to leave the area easily. If you'll be good enough to provide me with your contact information, perhaps we can all have another conversation later tonight."

Sanna provided the necessary information, and as they wrapped up their conversation, an issue crossed my mind. "How are we going to get back to our hotel? It's a long walk, and it looks like rain."

"Your mobiles should provide you with the necessary information for the bus routes." There wasn't any malice in his voice. The chief constable sounded like he was genuinely trying to be helpful.

"Can I get my umbrella?" Zabel asked. "It's… in… the.. boot." It was clear from the pauses in her voice and the expression on her face that not only did she know immediately that she wouldn't be allowed to take anything from the car, but she also probably wouldn't want the umbrella anymore given what it had touched.

Griogair confirmed what we both already knew, but just as he finished, Zabel remembered the additional contents of the boot. "Wait a minute. I had a lot of garment bags in there. What happened to my clothes?" She hurried back to the car. "I'm not going to touch anything. Just let me look from a distance." After staring at the open boot for about half a minute, she turned back to us, her face queasy but oddly relieved. "I don't see my garment bags. They took up a lot of space, so whoever put the bodies in the boot took them out. If you find my clothes, you'll find your killer."

"Whoever it was probably took out the umbrella, too," I noted. "Maybe we should wait a little while before buying a new one… or will you need it as evidence when you find it?"

"I'll need a description of the clothes and the umbrella," Griogair informed us.

"Sometimes as part of my work as a crime reporter, I have to change my clothes to better acclimate myself to a certain situation." Zabel was being very judicious with her choice of words.

"So basically, you pretend to be someone you're not in order to get information."

"There's no law against wearing an outfit connected to a job for which you are not actually gainfully employed."

"Unless you pretend to be a member of the police force."

"I have never done that and I don't own a policewoman's uniform. There are eight bags at the moment, all plastic-covered cloth. All different colors, it makes it easier to identify the items, but they're all labelled. There's a business suit, a carer's uniform, a white lab coat, a waitress's uniform... um... I'm blanking on the rest."

"A bag lady, a few fast-food uniforms from the leading franchises all in the same bag, an evening gown, and athletic wear," I completed.

"That's right. Good memory."

"And the umbrella's about three feet long– red, blue, yellow, and green with a ridged, curved wooden handle."

The young constable jotted down the necessary information.

"Well, I suppose that's all for now. I look forward to speaking to you again tonight." Griogair gave us a little nod. He started to turn away and then refocused his gaze towards us. "I really don't think that you had anything to do with this crime, you know. I wish you wouldn't be so suspicious of my motives in questioning you, but I can understand why you think that you might have to be on your guard with the police. But I have to stress, I'm not your enemy here."

I wanted to believe him, and frankly I wanted to get right to helping to solve the murders. Then I remembered that as civilians, we weren't supposed to investigate an open homicide ourselves, and as pleasant as the chief constable had been to us, he hadn't actually taken that last little step and invited us to partner with him in order to catch the killer. Indeed, Griogair doubled back and politely but sternly warned us not to play amateur detectives.

We agreed, trying hard to keep the disappointment out of our voices. After a minute of checking our mobiles, we discovered that a bus would arrive in just under a quarter of an hour. We'd have to get off four blocks from our hotel, but it was an easy walk. We walked for about six minutes to the bus stop.

My stomach started growling far louder than was polite, but I saw no disgust in Zabel's face, only the twitchiness she gets in her limbs when she's feeling hungry herself. The tattie scones and tea may have been tasty, but they didn't stick with her. We were already well past our lunchtime, and apparently she'd gotten over her queasiness after seeing the remains of the Monster Hunterz. Perhaps the ginger beer and mints were more effective than I'd initially thought. I checked my mobile again, and discovered that if the bus was on time, we *could* get to the hotel just before they stopped serving lunch. Assuming, of course that Abhorson wasn't feeling like he needed to take off early this afternoon, and he refused to serve us.

As we waited for our bus, Zabel had been staring off into space, playing with her watch, and humming softly, which meant that she had been thinking about something.

A chime from my phone told me that Sanna had sent me a text, saying that she was in a meeting right now, and that she'd call us in an hour.

Zabel didn't respond to this information immediately. She nodded without any indication she was really paying attention, and then, after another minute, she said, "It was more fun several months ago, when we were just investigating the theft of those letters to Sherlock Holmes, and the police didn't care about our trying to solve the case. I wonder... The chief constable told us that we couldn't pry into the murders, but he didn't say anything about trying to recover my missing clothes. The missing umbrella, too, for that matter."

"But that's pretty obvious, isn't it?"

"What do you mean?"

"I'm fairly certain that your clothes and umbrella are at the Hunniraube Manor. Unless of course, the thief/killer took them off the premises since we left."

Zabel looked at me for a few moments before nodding. "Wait a minute – I think that I understand now. There were only two opportunities for someone to break into my car, take out my clothes and umbrella, and hide the bodies. The first was when we were parked at the hotel. The second was at Hunniraube Manor. The hotel is a terrible place to break into a car. The car park there faces the street, and there are a couple of pubs across the street. Yeah, maybe someone would have had a chance to break in unobserved in the middle of the night, but I doubt it. But the Manor was a different situation. It was isolated, surrounded by trees and relatively private."

"I'm trying to find a subtle way to ask Philly if there's a deep freeze in the shed near where we parked."

"You think the bodies were hidden in that shed?"

"It makes sense. The killer wanted to get rid of them, but he – I'll use the masculine pronoun for convenience – also wanted them found in a place that wasn't connected to the Manor. I mean, why send a note to the police unless the killer– or at least, the person who moved the bodies – I'm assuming that they're the same person, but for all I know that may not be the case. So that leads to a few questions…"

I typed my questions down on my mobile as I spoke them for posterity.

"1. Why were the Monster Hunterz murdered, and when?

2. Why were their bodies frozen?

3. Are we correct about the bodies being kept in the shed at the Manor?

4. Why did someone who knew about the bodies decide to put them in Zabel's car?

5. Why did that person choose that moment to hide the bodies in the car, and not an earlier or later time?

6. Why did the killer send a note to the police, alerting them to the location of the corpses?

7. Why was it so vital that the bodies be discovered then by the police, and not by us at some point in the near future?

8. Was putting the bodies in Zabel's car a deliberate act of malice towards us, or was the car simply in the wrong place at the wrong time?

9. When the bodies were folded up before being frozen, was this simply so they'd fit in the deep freezes, or was the plan all along to put them in a car boot, and they needed to be arranged that way to fit the boot?"

I paused, trying to think of another question. I could only come up with one more:

"10. Who did this?"

"What do you think, Zabel?"

Before she could answer, the bus pulled up to our stop, and we hurried on, paid our fare, and found seats towards the back.

"I think you're asking exactly the right questions, Addy. I just can't think of answers that make any sense."

My mobile chimed again. Waldroup's slightly frantic voice answered my "Hello?"

"Addy? Waldroup here. I just heard about the Monster Hunterz. I need to talk to you. Where are you now?"

"Taking the bus back to our hotel. It'll be about fifteen minutes until we get there."

"Philly wants to see you, too. We'll be there in ten."

"Good. Go to the restaurant, please reserve a table for four, and please don't let the waiter say they've stopped serving. Tell him to keep the kitchen open for us."

"Easier said than done, but I'll try."

"Thanks. Have you heard the news about where the Hunterz were found?"

"Yes, and I have an idea about why they were there. I've got to go. Thanks for agreeing to talk to me. I'd hoped you weren't too upset about my dragging you into this."

"Oh, no. Always up for an adventure."

I'd held my mobile between my ear and Zabel's. "I wonder how a suspended constable found out about the bodies," she wondered. "Maybe he has a friend on the force who's keeping him informed."

"Sounds like a reasonable hypothesis." We brainstormed for another few minutes, before another chime informed me that Sanna was on the line.

"Addy? Tell Zabel I'll be there in time for a late dinner. I just booked two tickets for a flight to Inverness. Cheap ones, too."

"*Two* tickets?"

"Yes… Jasper's coming, too."

"What? Jasper's hardly left the flat in years, and now he's coming all the way up to Scotland?"

"I had to put a bit of pressure on him, but he agreed. We have mutual business interests. There's a potential scandal brewing, and I'm trying not to get burned by it."

"Wait a sec. Sanna, you know I'm an expert of crime thrillers, and I know that you need to hook your audience's interest, but you have to provide a little bit of context. What scandal? Are you in trouble?"

"Less so than you at the moment. I'll explain later. I have just enough time to get home and pack. Don't worry about me, worry about yourselves. Not so much about going to prison, I'm sure we'll be able to handle the situation with the police. If they thought you were guilty they'd never have let you leave in the first place. No, I'm worried about whoever it is that thought it would be a good idea to put bodies in Zabel's car. I think someone might have a grudge against her. Anyway, mull on that for a few hours until we see each other again."

After a brief pause, Zabel turned to me and said, "I do wonder, was putting the bodies in my car an act of malice or convenience?"

"Or maybe a little of both? I wonder –" My musings were interrupted by more chiming. My first thought was that Sanna was calling us back, but I was surprised to see it was my mother.

"Mum?"

"Addy! Why didn't you tell me right away you were in trouble? I thought I told you not to go playing amateur detective again, and look what happened!"

Realizing I was mumbling, I told her, "Well, I didn't plan for this to happen. We were just looking into what I thought was a harmless missing persons cases involving the Loch Ness Monster…"

"The Loch Ness Monster? Sweetheart, are you feeling all right?"

"It's a movie prop from a Sherlock Holmes movie, Mom. It'll make more sense when I tell you the whole story later."

"Are you coming home?"

"Well, no… The police won't let us. They don't suspect us of anything, but due to our proximity to the case we're not allowed to go." I decided to put the blame on the authorities in order to explain why I wasn't hurrying back to London. I wasn't about to head home until I knew just what was going on up here. Our tax pounds went to keep the police going, and I thought I might as well get my money's worth. Or did English taxpayers' money go to support the Scottish police, or were there fungibility issues? I wasn't sure on that point.

My thoughts on the fungibility of taxes collected in the United Kingdom was interrupted by Zabel joining in on the conversation. "Professor Zhuang?"

"Zabel, dear! Are you all right? Did you have a terrible shock?"

"Oh no, I wasn't badly shaken at all."

"Are you sure, dear? I heard that you were quite ill at the sight of the bodies."

I know mothers have a sixth sense about certain things, but even my mother's built-in concern radar isn't that finely tuned. "Mum, how did you know about all of this? It just happened. Please tell me this isn't on the news already. I didn't see any reporters around the police station."

"Oh no, of course not. My friend Sylvia teaches English at a school in Inverness. Her son is a police officer there – he's the one who helped open the boot of Zabel's car. Anyway, he left his inhaler at home this morning, so Sylvia popped down to the station to give it to him and he told her everything, and she recognized your names, so she got in touch with me immediately. I should text you her number, she'll probably want to invite you over for dinner. I'm sure that hotel food isn't very appetizing."

"Actually, it's very nice. The service leaves much to be desired, but you can't have everything." I suddenly remembered that Mum had been holding back on me lately. "Anyway, what right do you have for being upset that I didn't tell you about bodies being found in Zabel's car immediately? You've been keeping secrets from me. I know something's going on with you or with Dad, but you won't tell me."

"You're right, there is something, but I can't tell you about it now. It's nothing bad, don't worry. But you just have to wait another couple of days."

"Can't you just give me a hint, Mum?"

"No, any hint would give it away, and I'm afraid they'll find out and it'll spoil everything for your father. They might have our phone line tapped, you know, and they'll hear what I'm saying and punish Dad."

"Tapping your phone line? Mum, have you gotten on the wrong side of some branch of the government?"

"Don't worry about that, sweetheart. Everything's fine and under control. Just stay safe. By the way, shouldn't you have a solicitor present if they question you again?"

"Sanna's on her way here."

"Good, that's very good. Well, I have to go, but please, be careful. Stay safe, and don't worry about me."

"All right, but can you reciprocate and stop worrying about me as well?"

"I'm your mother, sweetheart. That's not how this works."

The goodbyes lasted about two minutes, and by that point we found it was time to get off the bus and hike back to the hotel. Abhorson met us at the dining room door with the level of geniality to which we were becoming accustomed, and he led us to a table where Waldroup and Philly were waiting for us. As we took our seats, Abhorson slapped menus on the table as if he was trying to swat flies.

"Oh no, we've already eaten," Philly said. "Just tea for us."

Well, I could have told her it wasn't wise to say something like that to Abhorson, but she didn't ask for my advice. "This is a restaurant, not a tea room. If you don't want to order a proper meal, then leave." In response to that command from their waiter, Waldroup and Philly picked up their menus in the meekest manner possible. The selection was quite a bit wider than what was offered last night for some reason, but it was still a very small menu.

Abhorson clearly did not believe in giving patrons enough time to read the menus more than once, though to be fair, we were calling it pretty close to the end of seating time.

"Mince and tatties," Waldroup ordered as if he were desperate for his waiter's approval.

"Small herb salad." Philly picked the lightest item that could potentially qualify as a meal. It came with a side order of disdain from Abhorson.

"The Brittanic coleslaw with chicken, please," said Zabel with a dazzling smile our waiter didn't deserve.

"I'll start with the bonfire warmer soup, followed by the locally smoked salmon with avocado fromage on the rye buttermilk bannocks, please." I wasn't one hundred percent sure what went into bonfire warmer soup, but it was a chilly, windy day and it sounded like the sort of dish that would work to raise my internal temperature by a substantial number of degrees.

"May I join you?" A man walked into the room, wearing an expensive-looking suit that had seen better days, and a dark brown overcoat in a similar state of repair. Though I'd never met him before, I deduced that he had to Lord Hunniraube's brother Lachlan, due to the strong resemblance. Lachlan looked very similar to his brother, but the main difference was that Lachlan looked substantially less likely to attack you with a double-bladed axe while you slept.

"Uncle Lachlan! What are you doing here?"

Before he had a chance to respond to Philly's question, Abhorson cut in and informed him, "If you join them, you have to eat with them."

"Ah... er..." I handed him my menu, and after taking ten seconds longer than Abhorson desired, he selected "The barbecued piggy scallops starter."

As our waiter returned to the kitchen without bringing a chair for our new guest, I rose and fetched one from the empty table nearest to us. As soon as he sat down, he explained, "Philly, we need to talk about your father."

"What has he done now?"

"The police just arrived at the manor, and they're making a full search. One of them commented that your father owned a few too many weapons, and I'm afraid the situation devolved from there. If I hadn't been right there to hold him back he'd have thrown a punch at one of the constables."

"Oh, no."

"At least he wasn't directing that punch at me," Waldroup said with a weak smile.

"Not the time, Droopy."

"Sorry, darling." He ran his hand over his girlfriend, and she actually cooed at him. It made me rather uncomfortable. Don't get me wrong, I like it when Zabel expresses warmth towards me, but I prefer it in private. Public displays of affection just unsettle me a bit. Also, at that moment I was once again eternally grateful that Zabel had never seen fit to bestow a sappy nickname upon me, like "Droopy." At university, I once talked to a very attractive woman at a party, and after only four minutes of conversation, she called me "Addy-Waddy-Daddy." I knew at once that no good could come of any relationship with her, so I excused myself, telling her I needed to refresh my drink. I wound up grabbing my coat and leaving for home at ten minutes to eight. I really don't care for noisy, crowded parties anyway.

"So, may I call you Lachlan?" Zabel asked.

"Please do."

"Thank you. Lachlan, your niece asked you a question. What are you doing here? Please don't get me wrong, we're certainly pleased to meet you and happy to share a meal with you, but I'm just curious…"

Lachlan nodded. "Yes, of course. I should explain. The police arrived at the manor a little while ago. As you probably surmised from my comments a minute ago, my dear brother has been in one of his… distinctive moods. He chose to interpret some of the perfectly reasonable questions the police posed as impertinent, and he threw quite the fit."

"Did you give him one of those shots to calm him down?" Philly asked, making no effort to hide the anxiety in her voice.

"Yes. I must say, it was rather lucky that his sciatica's been acting up lately. It made it harder for him to dodge the hypodermic needle. He still managed to bob and weave a bit, but I managed to pin him against the wall and administer the medication. He's lying comfortably in bed now, and I made sure to lock him in his room."

"Is he safe in there? Couldn't he do some sort of harm to himself?" I asked.

"Ah, I forgot to mention. There's a one-way unbreakable glass panel in the room, and we have a full-time nurse on staff. She's watching him now, and if there's any trouble she'll pop in and take care of everything. I need to remind her to refill Daddy's prescription for beta-blockers. I'd bet five pounds she's already done it, actually. She's very efficient, very good at her job."

"And built like a rugby player, too," Waldroup added. "In case you were worried, she can handle him easily."

"That's nice to know," I replied. "Does he have any weapons in his room?"

"No, we made sure everything's in the hall. It took a lot of negotiation, but we finally sorted that out as a compromise."

"Don't be so sure," Philly warned. "The other day, I went into his room to make sure he hadn't been eating scones and marmalade in bed again – last time he attracted so many bugs with all the crumbs – anyway, I found a dagger underneath his pillow."

Lachlan sagged in his chair. "I didn't check for hidden weapons. For all I know he's got a crossbow under his mattress."

"Oh, dear. Well, Nurse Bulstrode will catch him if she sees anything."

Zabel pressed forward – I could tell that her journalistic instincts had been whetted, and she knew that there was more to the story. "But that's can't be the only reason why you came all the way down here. You could have just called Philly to let her know what was happening at the manor."

"Quite right. I must admit, I had multiple motives here. First, I wanted to meet the two of you. I heard that you were invited here, and rumour says it was Waldroup who called you up here, but no one's bothered to tell me all the details."

We provided him with a concise story of how we came up here, and by the time we were finished, Abhorson arrived with our food. He served Zabel first, then Philly, then Lachlan, then Waldroup and finally finished with me. "I brought you your soup along with your entrée, as no one else ordered more than one course, and I didn't think you wanted to stuff your face while the rest of your table had nothing." He stabbed me in the face with his gaze, daring me to contradict him. Frankly, I was fine with being served in this manner, but the look on his face made me almost wish to find a fly or something in my soup, just so I could have a little something to point out that he was not so perfect himself.

Once again, the service left much to be desired, but the food itself made up for the staffing issues. Apparently, bonfire warmer soup was a curried chicken cream base with vegetables, and it was certainly effective at dispelling the chill that had seeped through my coat and under my skin. I had no complaints about the salmon and avocado cheese spread either, although upon reflection, I realized I would have preferred a hot entrée. At least the bannocks – little circular flatbreads – tasted as if they were fresh from the oven.

Looking around the table, "barbecued piggy scallops" was just another way of saying "bacon-wrapped scallops." "Mince and tatties" was Scottish for seasoned ground beef and mashed potatoes. Philly's herb salad looked pretty on the plate – glistening greens with a sprinkling of brightly colored vegetables – but it looked unsubstantial, more of a garnish than an actual meal or even a starter, sparsely arranged.

I had expected Zabel's Brittanic coleslaw to be shredded cabbage with a little Union Jack on it , but she later informed me there were also apples, other crisp vegetables, sour cream, and some sort of pale cheese she couldn't identify but liked, though she wasn't going to ask Abhorson what it was out of principle.

My hunger was stronger than my curiosity, and I started eating rather than asking questions. Zabel, in contrast, had her reporter instincts at full power, and she only took a bite of her coleslaw before asking, "So, Lachlan, you say that the police are at the manor? Do you know what they're doing there?"

"Thankfully, they're not questioning the guests or the speakers. Not yet, at any rate. They're taking a look around the manor, but they're not taking anything at this point. They're thawing out the bodies so that they can perform the autopsies, from what I overheard. They can't take any of the swords or axes or daggers until they know for sure that those two men were stabbed or something like that, but they are photographing everything and checking for any spaces indicating a missing weapon. Of course, there's no reason to assume that they were killed with one of the items from my brother's collection, but when there's a full-fledged armory on the property, I can't blame them for casting suspicious eyes in that direction. But they're not that interested in the manor, except for the kitchen."

"Why are they interested in our kitchen?" Philly wondered. "Is it because they think we might have violated some sort of health and safety standard?"

"No, it's because the bodies were frozen solid," Zabel explained. "I believe they want to see if your kitchen freezers might have been used for that purpose."

"No chance of that," Lachlan assured us. "Our walk-in freezers are full of food, with no place to hide a body. The kitchen staff uses them several times a day. There's no way the corpses of two grown men could have been hidden there without being discovered. But there is another possibility, as I told the authorities when they queried about any freezers we might have on the premises. There's that little shed off to the side of the property."

"The one in the grove of trees, with the green roof and brown walls, with a handful of parking spaces to one side?" I asked.

"Yes. You've seen it?"

"We were parked there today," Zabel explained. "Addy and I had a theory that the only opportunity someone might have had to plant the bodies in my car was when we parked at that out-of-the-way spot at the manor. And as someone wasn't likely to make two trips, walking from, say, the kitchen to my car with a body slung over that person's shoulder, it seems much more likely that the bodies were hidden in the shed."

"That is a possibility," Lachlan agreed. "An unsettlingly likely one, actually. There's a pair of deep freezes in that shed. Fairly large ones, actually. If you took out most of what was in there, both of them would hold a medium-sized body. If the body was folded up so the head was against the knees, I suppose."

"What do you keep in there?" Zabel asked.

"*I* don't keep anything in them. They're where my dear brother keeps his Nessie bait. The treats that he's convinced are going to catch the Loch Ness Monster. Over the years, he's wasted hundreds of pounds of bacon –"

Zabel interrupted. "He said that bacon wouldn't work."

"Yes, he came to that conclusion through trial and error. He's tried steaks, leg of lamb, chicken, geese, turkeys, hams, huge bunches of spinach, root vegetables, even a huge seriously strong cheddar cheese."

I'd never heard of seriously strong cheddar cheese before, but at that moment I really wanted some.

"Nothing worked," Lachlan continued. "He's tried all these different kinds of fish, like salmon, kippers… smoked or fresh. He's even used shrimps and lobsters. Nessie eats better than I do! At least, the Loch Ness

Monster *would*, if it actually existed and ever actually tried to take a bite out of any of the delicacies it offers. But it never has, of course."

"He told us that he'd ordered fifty pounds of sardines," I noted. After a moment of silent thought, I wondered if he'd meant fifty pounds of sardines in terms of weight, or if he'd meant he'd paid fifty pounds of cash money on sardines. Either way, I thought that Lord Hunniraube was making his fishmonger very happy.

"Yes, he was told it would take a bit of time to fulfill his order, as he wanted fresh sardines. He can't stand opening up tins. He's cut himself on the sharp lids a couple of times, and he's become a bit phobic about them. He'd spent the last couple of days clearing out the deep freezes to make room for all of the sardines, using the contents to set his Nessie traps. Or rather, he had *me* lug all the frozen fish fingers and whatnot to the shore of the loch. Nothing ever happens to them, and I always have to throw them away after they've sat there for days. Such a wicked waste."

"So there was plenty of room in the deep freezes," Zabel mused.

"Yes. We also keep some pry bars and screwdrivers and other tools there, so I suppose something might have been used to open up the boot of your car. I am genuinely sorry to hear about that. If something like that did happen on our property, please let me find some way to make the situation right." Lachlan seemed deeply upset by the fact that Zabel's car might have been befouled by bodies on his family's property.

Zabel seemed appreciative. "I need to check with my insurance company. I have no idea if they cover replacements to a vehicle if it's still functional but you never want to use the boot again."

"I can recommend an excellent crime scene cleaner," Waldroup offered.

"I don't think any amount of scrubbing or bleach will make me feel comfortable using that car ever again, but I appreciate the thought, thank you."

"There's a friend of mine in Aberdeen, he sells used cars in excellent condition. If you feel like going over there, he might be able to set you up with a very reasonable deal." From the expression on his face, Lachlan felt bad about what happened to Zabel's car, but he wasn't in any hurry to take out his checkbook and square accounts by actually buying her another car himself. Especially since Zabel had just shot down the offer of a nice, inexpensive spray of disinfectant in the boot and calling it good as new.

Philly cut into the conversation. "Look, the reason why we came here is because we wanted all the details on what happened. If the police are right and the bodies were put into your car at the manor... Well, that's very unsettling to me. I need to know if Daddy... could be getting worse and if he might have... crossed the line. Please, could we hear the story of what happened from your perspective? It would really help me know what to do with Daddy."

Zabel made a little face. She likes to be the one who asks the questions, but there was no way to gracefully escape the situation – we might as well just assuage their curiosity. Really, it could have been an investment. The more we told them, the more willing they might be to respond to our inquiries.

After a quick glance at each other and silently confirming that we were on the same page, Zabel and I tag-teamed and told them a condensed story of our afternoon. By the time we'd finished our narrative, our plates were clean. Lachlan had eaten all of his piggy scallops as well, but Waldroup had left a fair portion of his mince and tatties behind, and Philly, who had ordered the least amount of food, had also consumed the smallest amount. When Lachlan asked Abhorson to wrap up his leftovers, our waiter responded as if he'd been asked to climb Mount Everest and bring back a handful of snow.

"You'll be having something for afters, of course." Abhorson made a statement. He didn't ask a question.

"Ooh! Do you have your tablet?" I thought at first Waldroup was referring to an electronic device, but as he informed me right afterwards, Scottish tablet is a fudge-like confection, a little crumblier, made with condensed milk, butter, and sugar, and usually flavored with vanilla. Waldroup nodded, and without asking the rest of us, ordered a small plate of tablet for the table.

It arrived in seconds, as it wasn't particularly difficult to prepare. With a name like "tablet," I was expecting little pills. Instead, it was five squares, two inches to a side, and an inch thick, all a pleasant golden-brown color. It was a very nice sweet, but I prefer chocolate fudge.

After her first little nibble, Zabel asked, "Is there any news on my clothes?"

"Not to my knowledge," Lachlan replied, "but the police haven't been telling me much."

"Thank you for meeting us. We were desperate to hear exactly what had happened with the Monster

Hunterz." Philly only took two small bites of her tablet before giving the lion's share to Waldroup. "We really ought to get back. We need to oversee the late afternoon group flash fiction writing sessions. I hope the police can confirm that no dead bodies have been in our kitchen freezers, otherwise the guests might demand that we order pizzas for dinner. And our budget is so tight, we can't afford to waste any food."

"How long have the guests been at the manor?" I asked.

Lachlan took a moment to think, and then replied, "We're getting towards the end of a two-week writing session. The five authors arrived ten days ago, right before the Monster Hunterz first appeared – I believe they came to town the next day. One group of guests stayed for one week, and then they left and the Week Two guests arrived."

That meant that none of the guests was likely to have been involved in the crime, just the staff, the writers, Lord Hunniraube, and the people sitting with us. As if he read my mind, Waldroup confirmed my ruling out the guests, and added, "Not only that, but based on my own discreet inquiries, all of the lodge staff was working in groups to cook and clean while you were at the lodge today, and Lord Hunniraube's nurse was in town picking up some medication. That means the only people at the scene who could have moved the bodies into your car were the three writers you met – the other two were in a seminar and have an alibi – Lord Hunniraube, Philly, and Lachlan, and I can vouch for Philly and Lachlan. They're not murderers."

"And the writers have no motive for killing them," Philly added. "I'm very much afraid that Daddy was involved." She didn't *look* too afraid of this possibility. I rather think that she hated the thought that her father might be dangerous, but she was rather hoping that the authorities might take him away to someplace reasonably humane where he'd be looked after and she'd be free to live her own life.

"But why would your father attack them?" Zabel asked.

"Because of Nessie, of course! They were trying to track the Loch Ness Monster down, and Daddy must have flipped out at the thought of someone else getting to it before he did. Don't you see, it's the only possible motive? None of the rest of us have any semblance of a reason to kill them, and neither do any of the writers."

Philly really wants us to believe that her father killed them, I thought to myself. As I wondered why, Abhorson delivered the check and Lachlan snatched it up with a firm, "Please, allow me." We thanked him, but our efforts to ask some more questions were thwarted by Philly continuing to chatter about how concerned she was about her father and hoping that he would get the help he'd needed for quite some time.

"What do you plan to do for this evening?" Waldroup asked.

I hadn't really thought about it, but I realized that our options were limited. We no longer had a car for travelling, and Chief Constable Griogair probably wouldn't look too kindly at our showing up at the manor.

I explained this point, and Lachlan nodded. "That makes sense to me. We would have invited you to the manor for dinner, but you're right – it's wisest for you to stay away, assuming that the police are still there."

"We'll probably stay here at the hotel and work on some notes for an upcoming video," Zabel added.

"Sounds like a good plan," Lachlan said. "I'd suggest you catching a film at the theatre within walking distance down the street, but it's looking like heavy rain is coming, and you don't want to catch a cold after getting drenched."

As Waldroup started to leave, I asked him why the police thought he was involved in a fraud with the Monster Hunterz.

"Oh, that. I printed out everything I could find on the Internet about the lost Nessie prop, and my peers found it. They started asking me if I was going to help the Hunterz fake the Monster's presence, and I panicked. I suppose I blew it all out of proportion." I nodded, but I couldn't help but think his casualness seemed overdone.

We said our goodbyes, and the other three headed out into the rapidly darkening afternoon.

Zabel gathered up an armload of notes from her room, and we sat down in a couple of comfy chairs in a corner of the hotel and attempted to work on an upcoming script. Not surprisingly, our minds were so filled with the events of the last few hours that we were unable to concentrate, and by evening, we had produced no more than a couple of sentences of usable work.

Around sunset, the storm broke and rain started pouring down so hard I started to worry that it would poke holes in the hotel roof. Another text from Sanna told us that they had landed safely and they'd arrive at the hotel within the hour, assuming they could find a taxi. Zabel and I pretty much gave up any hopes of being productive, and we gathered up our papers and instead played a couple of little wooden puzzle games that had been left on a shelf in the lounge. They did nothing to take our minds off the case.

After a little while, we started hearing a particularly sharp argument coming from outside the window, and I recognized both voices. Sanna and Jasper both have excellent lungs, and they managed to make their asperity heard even over the sound of the wind and the rain.

We hurried to the main door and let them in, getting a splatter of precipitation in our faces as a reward. Sanna and Jasper were both soaked to the skin, and from their scowls, it was pretty clear that it was more than just the weather that got to them.

"What's wrong?" I asked, knowing as I said it that it was a waste of breath. No force on earth could hold back Sanna from complaining, and she was about to tell us what had happened. There was no need to ask.

"I'll tell you what's bloody wrong," she snapped. "I just got fired, and I think that your pal Lord Hunniraube is to blame."

CHAPTER SIX
Peerage Maker

"You two are dripping all over the carpet," Zabel noted. There was no chastising in her voice, it was simply a statement of fact, and neither of them was annoyed by her tone.

"Not surprising. I feel like I've been dropped into Loch Ness." Sanna stepped over to the side and wrung out the bottom half of her coat over a potted plant that threatened to take over the main hall in a couple of years. Meanwhile, Jasper peeled off his mackintosh and threw it over an empty coatrack.

"Good thing I packed all of my recording equipment in a hard-shelled suitcase," Jasper commented. "It's supposed to be waterproof, but I'm going to need to check."

"We'll need a couple of rooms."

"Didn't you book them already?" I asked Sanna.

"I've got a lot on my mind lately." She crossed the hall to the front desk and started pounding the little bell, obviously relishing the small but cathartic sense of relief that came with every chime. After a couple of minutes, the tiny elderly woman reappeared, this time wearing a sky-blue blouse. When she finally made it to the desk, she looked up at Sanna.

"Are you here for dinner?"

"Yes, but I want to book two rooms."

"Oh, I'm afraid we're all full."

"They only have six rooms here at the Maroon Unicorn," I added.

Sanna whirled around at me. "It'd have been nice if you'd told me that ahead of time, Zhuang."

"I thought you were sufficiently organized to handle your own travel plans. Anyway, I've been kind of distracted thanks to the double homicide. Remember that?"

"I am NOT going out in that rain again," Sanna snapped.

"Looks like we'll have to all bunk in one room," Jasper shrugged. "I hope none of you mind my snoring."

"We have two rooms," Zabel informed him.

"Two?"

"If you spent a little less time in your room talking with your idiot friends about television shows you all hate, you would have noticed that when Zabel comes to the flat, she heads back to her own home well before bedtime," Sanna snapped.

I know it was nothing to be ashamed of at all, but I was uncomfortable with Jasper and Sanna providing details of my relationship with Zabel in front of the desk clerk. I didn't want her gossiping with Abhorson later.

Sanna turned to Zabel, "It looks like I'll be rooming with you. Do you mind?"

"Not at all."

"Then Addy, you'll be rooming with Jasper. I pity you."

I wasn't sure why the prospect of sharing a room with Jasper filled me with nameless dread, but it did. Much like Zabel, Jasper makes his living as a YouTuber, and he's been known to spend as much as ten hours a day livecasting, and the rest of his waking hours recording and editing videos. His room in our flat is soundproofed, and he rarely leaves it except for meals. Come to think of it, I couldn't think of a time when he'd left the flat at all in the past year, although who knows what he does when Sanna and I at work. Still, it must have taken something very important in order to compel him to make the trip all the way up to Scotland.

Even though I'd never heard him thanks to the soundproofing, I had the sense that Jasper was a heavy snorer. He just gives that impression.

Perhaps he sensed my reluctance, because Jasper slapped me on the back with a very damp hand. "No need to look so apprehensive, mate. I've got a livestream with some of my pals from Florida and Texas tonight. I won't keep you up. Is there a room here I can use? That lounge over there? Do they have a spare conference room? I could probably make do with a broom closet if necessary. I just need to check the acoustics. They won't be up to my usual standards, but when I explain that I'm visiting Loch Ness, I don't think my audience will mind."

"I still don't believe that people pay good money to hear you rant and complain about how Hollywood is ruining all of your favorite franchises."

"I make more than you, Sanna."

"You keep saying that, but I have yet to see your tax forms."

"Will there be anything else?" asked the tiny elderly desk clerk.

"Yes. Two more keys for us." The clerk complied, and then tottered into the back room without another word.

Sanna turned to us. "I need to change, assuming that any of my clothes are dry."

"And I need to check my equipment. As well as change into fresh clothes."

By this time, the dining room was already full, as a local family was holding a birthday party for a grandparent. We were, however, informed that they could seat us in the tiny private room off to the side if we were willing to wait about an hour for the current occupants of the room to finish their meal. Both of them brought nearly as much luggage as Zabel, so we helped them carry everything upstairs.

In my– or rather our– room, Jasper poked the mattress with a cautious finger. "This is a little soft for me. And are those down pillows?" He pulled out the tag and gave it a careful glance. "I'm allergic to feathers." This was the first I'd ever heard about that. It was amazing that we could have been flatmates for so long and I there was so much I didn't know about him. Come to think of it, I realized that I wasn't quite sure what Jasper's last name was. And by this point, it would have been far too awkward to ask. Maybe at some point he'd leave his wallet alone and I could check it.

Jasper started feeling a recliner in one corner. "This is better for me. I'll sleep in this chair. I usually sleep better seated anyway."

"I didn't know that." I think I'd only been in Jasper's room twice since we started sharing a flat. Due to the background curtains he hung up during filming his videos, I couldn't see if he had an actual bed in there or not.

"Oh yeah, ever since I herniated a disk playing rugby."

"I wasn't aware you were an athlete."

"Well, not for years," he replied, patting his belly. "But as a teen, I was a great sportsman, not to brag. I thought about going pro as a footballer, but my injuries threw that out the window. I often wonder what my life would've been like if I'd been able to follow my initial sports dreams."

"Why am I only learning about this now? We've been friends since university."

"Well, I just don't care to talk about it too much. It's a painful subject. Quite literally, really. Enough of the road not taken for now." He fiddled with a little number lock and he flipped open one suitcase, then repeated the process three times. "Ah, good. Everything looks totally dry. Including my clothes."

As he changed, I looked out the window as the storm wreaked havoc on the trees. The winds made the branches swing back and forth like windshield wipers, and the droplets smacking the pane of glass, sounding like a machine gun firing.

"Addy! You've got to try this!" I turned around to see that Jasper had traded his soaked dark blue sweatshirt and grey sweatpants for a green sweatshirt and black sweatpants, as well as dry socks and trainers. I have never seen him wear an outfit that didn't consist of sweats. At university, one of our professors passed away after a brief illness, and at the memorial service, Jasper work a black sweatshirt and sweatpants. Whenever he's questioned about this, he makes it clear that according to his personal sense of fashion, comfort triumphs over everything. Frankly, I totally sympathize with him.

Shoving a plastic bottle in my hands, Jasper explained, "It's Irn-Bru! It's a soda. I discovered it at the airport. Try it."

I'm not particularly fond of soft drinks, but he seemed so enthusiastic it seemed rude not to try it. I unscrewed the cap, poured a tiny bit into a glass on the sideboard so as not to feel obligated to finish the whole bottle after putting it in my mouth, and took a sip of the bright orange beverage. I expected it to taste like orange, and I definitely got little hints of that fruit, but I also picked up banana and some kind of sugary candy. I mentioned this, and added, "I'm also tasting... something rusty."

"That's why they call it Irn-Bru, I guess. They call it "Scotland's other national drink.""

"Other than what?"

"Whisky."

"Yeah, that sounds right."

"What do you think?"

"It's... not my favorite, but I'm glad I've been trying lots of new things since I came up here." I handed the open bottle back to him, hoping that his newly acquired taste for it would compel him to finish it off himself, and fortunately, this proved to be the case.

Jasper took a huge swig of the Irn-Bru. "I was so thirsty after the flight, and I overheard a couple of other people at the airport commenting on how much they liked it. So I bought a bottle, chugged it down, and enjoyed it so much I bought another. By the time I was halfway through my third bottle, I was hooked, but Sanna said we had to keep going. I purchased a few more bottles, just in case I couldn't find it anywhere handy."

"Who told you it was one of Scotland's national drinks?"

"The clerk at the store. I wonder if you can buy it in London. I don't remember ever seeing it, but then again, I haven't been in many shops lately." Jasper prefers to have his food and other supplies delivered to the flat. He keeps up his busy schedule of recording videos with a steady stream of energy drinks and caffeinated beverages– mostly sodas.

Jasper raved about the Irn-Bru for a few more minutes, like an oenophile raving about a particularly fine French wine, punctuating his surprisingly eloquent review with deep swigs of the beverage. Right after he drained the bottle dry, I suggested that it was time to go down to dinner. As we walked, I asked him, "So, do you know what's going on with Sanna's job?"

"Yes. It's connected with one of my sponsors. Peerage Maker."

I don't have nine hours a day to spare watching Jasper's videos and livestreams, but the sponsor jogged a memory. "I vaguely remember you mentioning it, but when I watch your videos I tend to fast forward through the commercials."

"Well, Peerage Maker–"

"Eh! Eh! Eh! Eh!" Sanna and Zabel had emerged from their room. "Not in public! Wait until we're someplace where we're sure no one else will overhear!" Sanna was wearing her pajamas and a brightly-colored dressing gown. Seeing my expression, she explained, "The rain seeped through my suitcase and soaked everything except these. They were rolled up in the center and stayed dry, aside from a little dampness on the bottom hem."

"And my hairdryer took care of that. We hung up everything else, and it should be dry by morning." Zabel said that soothingly, clearly trying to calm her down. I suddenly realized that Abhorson had better be on his best behavior. If he got snotty with Sanna, he might well need a neck brace. Zabel, incidentally, had also changed her clothes for dinner, even though her outfit hadn't gotten wet. She was now wearing a long red dress and matching cardigan, and she looked even more fantastic than usual.

We made our way towards the dining room, where about thirty people were talking at a volume that made it clear that alcohol was definitely being served, and it was probably an open bar. A young woman in a uniform that was a couple of sizes too big for her informed us that the private dining room was ready, and asked us to follow her. Explaining that she didn't usually work here, but she was hired for the party, she noted that she'd had to borrow a uniform from Abhorson. She seemed self-conscious about her appearance as Sanna had a belligerent expression, as if she were daring someone to make a comment about wearing her sleepwear.

And comment someone did. The door to the little dining room was right next to one of the kitchen doors, and just as we were about to enter, Abhorson popped out the door, holding a large covered tray. He gave Sanna a chilly up-and-down glance, and snapped, "Our dress code forbids patrons from wearing their pajamas at the restaurant."

Without missing a beat, Sanna barked, "This is the national costume of my ancestors, you xenophobic, racist toad. If you bar me from service I'll file a discrimination grievance with the Equality and Human Rights Commission, and when I'm done with you, you won't be able to get a job better than scrubbing out the oil residue from the deep-fryer at Wimpy's with your hair."

Abhorson didn't even flinch, "Even then, my hair would look less greasy than–"

"Hey! What are you doing standing around out there? They're waiting for their entrees!" A chef poked her head out the kitchen. "Hurry it up!"

Sanna and Abhorson both muttered something undiscernible but aggressive-sounding, and he marched off to the dining room with his dignity undamaged, and Sanna strode into the little dining room like a queen. A queen who was a hair's breath away from punching out an underling. It was really a booth, with the plush benches lining three sides of the square room, with a circular table in the middle. "I'll be with you in a moment," our waitress assured us. "Please note that we're serving a limited menu based upon the food being served at the party." She placed four postcard-sized menus on the table, smiled, and shut the folding doors. Fortunately, the doors had large glass panes, otherwise it might have felt a bit claustrophobic.

"What's the matter?" Zabel asked me. "You look pensive."

"For some reason, I suddenly have the feeling that I've seen Abhorson somewhere before here, but I can't remember where. But it has something to do with our big adventure several months ago."

"He can't have served at one of the restaurants where we've eaten. I'm sure I would have remembered that."

"I would have, too. For some reason, I don't think we *met* him before, but I saw his picture somewhere…"

"Perhaps he was in the newspaper. I wouldn't be surprised he got arrested for something obscene," Sanna suggested.

"This is going to bother me all night…" I mused.

Squinting at the little card, Sanna said, "I can't read the menu. The lights aren't strong and the print is tiny."

"They specialize in traditional Scottish dishes here," Zabel explained. "For starters, the only option is cock-a-leekie soup–"

"I'm not eating anything that sounds like men's incontinence problems."

"It's chicken–"

"I know what it is, and I want none of it."

Jasper and I had no such compunction.

There were only two options for the entrée – the vegetarian option of Scottish potato pie, and a Scottish steak pie. Both were designed to serve two, so we decided to order one of each and split them among ourselves.

Once our order had been placed and the doors closed again, I asked, 'So, what exactly is Peerage Maker?"

"They wrote to me a couple of months ago, offering to sponsor one of my videos," Zabel recalled. "Their terms seemed pretty generous, but I never accept advertising without doing a full background check. My sources wouldn't go into specifics, but they said to be wary of them because something didn't smell right, so I turned them down."

"You were smarter than him." Sanna jabbed a finger in Jasper's direction.

"And apparently smarter than Sanna's bosses as well," Jasper retorted.

"Yes, how did you get fired?" I asked.

"I'll get to that all in good time. I'll make it fast. Peerage Maker is a company for people who are sick and tired on being called just plain 'Mr.' or 'Mrs.' but haven't got the brains to get a doctorate or the strength to move up the ranks in the military. The company professes that they can make anybody a member of the Scottish aristocracy simply by coughing up some cash."

"And how does that work? Do they get adopted by a nobleman?"

"Not even close. Apparently, there's supposedly some tradition in Scotland where if you own a certain amount of land in a certain place, then hey presto, that automatically makes you a member of the titled nobility, and you can call yourself Lord Such-and-Such or Lady Whoopty-doo. So, Peerage Maker offers people to buy as little as one square inch of land, and in return, you're supposedly granted the right to slap Lord or Lady before your name."

"That doesn't sound right to me," I said. "I don't claim to know very much about the inner workings of the upper crust, but I do know that it's not that easy to become a member of that group without doing something impressive or profitable for the powers that be, or marrying into the titled classes. A lot of the old aristocratic families were either successful knights or major land owners centuries ago. Plenty of them got their titles for doing Henry VIII's bidding and beating up a bunch of monks and stealing their abbeys. If everybody who owned their own vegetable gardens in Scotland got to title themselves 'Lord' or 'Lady,' the House of Lords would be packed as tightly as a can of sardines."

"Exactly." Sanna nodded. "See, Jasper? Doesn't that makes sense to you? Or did they dangle so much advertising money in front of you that your critical thinking skills took the year off?"

"Once again, I admit that I swallowed everything hook, line, and sinker, but I'm not the only one. So many of my YouTube peers were promoting them, I assumed that everything was legit."

Sanna sniffed. "Your peers. Your livestreaming peers are a motley crew who play video games twelve hours a day, but you think that all of that life experience rescuing princesses from castles will teach you how to spot a scam."

Jasper groaned and turned to Zabel and me for sympathy. "She was like this the whole flight up here. And once again, I'd like to point out that law school also failed to raise any red flags for your colleagues."

"Wait, I'm going to need some more clarification," Zabel said. "What exactly is the con here?"

"Well, essentially, people are paying Peerage Maker money for nothing, or at least, nothing much. If you read the contract carefully, Peerage Maker isn't actually selling people postage stamp-sized plots of land. They say they're signing over the title to the land, but the legalese basically says that they're selling people the right to *say* that they own those little bits of land. They're not allowed to grow any crops or build anything on the land. Though what you could build on a little patch of dirt like that is beyond me. A flagpole? Actually, someone who thought they had bought tiny bits of land nearby could claim that the shadow of a flagpole was devaluing their property. And even if someone bought enough adjoining microplots to have space for a cottage or something, well, they still wouldn't have the right to actually put up a building. Anyway, they have a clause in the contract that says if anybody wants to sell their land – or at least, the right to *claim* one owns the land – Peerage Maker has the right of first refusal to buy it back for a fraction of the original selling price. Anyway, just to prevent any claims, they set up policies so if people buy, say, a square foot of land, it's to be sold in the most unusual way possible. Instead of a square one foot by one foot, they'll assign them a plot one inch by one hundred forty-four inches. Same amount of land, but arranged in such a way it's completely worthless. Not that you could do much with a square foot, anyway. What could you do with a plot shaped like that?"

"Grow spaghetti?" Jasper chuckled.

Sanna sent him a death glare. "Aren't you hilarious? So basically, Peerage Maker is not-really selling people barely enough dirt to grow a daisy, and telling people that they are now a lord or a lady. They're nothing of the kind, of course. Because the whole premise of buying land and then getting a title of nobility is a crock and a half. Simply owning land isn't enough to get the legal right to slap a title at the front of your name. That's not how they do things in Scotland, or anywhere, for that matter. The company has misstated the legal requirements for lordship or ladyship. People think they've bought their way up the social ladder for a few dozen pounds, but in reality they've gained nothing and poked a hole in their own wallets."

"Surely there can't be much money in selling one-inch square plots of land," Zabel mused.

"Not very much, no. But that's not where the real profits are. Peerage Maker rakes in the big pounds by selling framed certificates declaring that person a titled lord or lady, and registration fees for people who design their own coats of arms and family mottos. Cough up a few hundred pounds, get a piece of paper that says "I'm a sucker.""

"How many people fell for it?" I asked.

"Enough so that the profits run into the millions," Sanna replied. "It's a low-expense business. All you have to do is pick up some fancy paper, a printer, and some fancy cheap frames, and everything else is money in the bank. Cough up some loot, and suddenly you're the Duke of Dumbarton. Apparently it's very popular in countries that have no idea how the British peerage system really works. Of course, none of this would be possible if people like Jasper didn't promote the scam to millions of their viewers, and for the ten thousandth time, how you can possibly get over 2 million viewers for one of your silly videos is beyond me."

"Well, now I know how the company works, but how does that affect your job?" I asked Sanna.

"Ah. As you know, until very recently, I was employed to handle some of the civil work for a moderately sized entertainment firm. And apparently my bosses are in the habit of joining forces with all of these fledgling companies that they think are cool. My company apparently represents Peerage Maker, although I wasn't aware of this until a couple of days ago, when my supervisor told me to look into some projects – I can't go into details because I'm still bound by some confidentiality rules, but the long and the short of the matter is, I smelt a rat, and pointed it out to my superiors, who freaked out, because being connected to an unethical scheme like this would shatter their precious, precious reputations. I didn't care much for the idea of hushing everything up, so voices were raised, some insults may have been thrown –"

"By you," Jasper interrupted.

Ignoring him, Sanna continued, "and the long and the short of it is, I no longer have a job. I may or may not receive a nice severance package, depending on whether or not I'm willing to sign a non-disclosure agreement that forces me to shut up and let people keep believing that it's perfectly all right to send the grocery money to Peerage Maker if they decide they'd rather be a member of the upper crust than buy a crust of bread to eat."

"They say it's really meant as a gag gift," Jasper argued.

"A whoopie cushion or a rubber chicken is a gag gift. Peerage Maker is money for nothing. Besides, lots of people are thinking they're buying peerages for themselves. Are you saying they're pranking themselves? And I seem to recall you saying at dinner the other night that I'd have to start calling you "Lord Jasper Portendorfer" from now on."

Portendorfer! That was Jasper's last name! He certainly mustn't have ever mentioned it to me. I would have remembered it if he had.

Zabel, who showed no signs of surprise at hearing our friend's surname, said, "I don't remember you mentioning that."

"You and Addy were out on a date that night. You'd be surprised at the conversations the two of us have when you're not around."

I nodded. "I'm starting to realize that I'm missing out on a lot of what's going on in the lives of my flatmates."

"It's not that interesting. We argue a lot about the shows and movies Jasper uses as the subjects of his videos."

"Even if she hasn't seen them, she has very strong opinions about them," Jasper noted.

Sanna sniffed. "I don't need go down into the sewer to smell it."

Feeling the need to backtrack, I tried to redirect the conversation. "So essentially, Peerage Maker is acting really shady by taking money and saying people can proclaim an honorific that they actually don't have any legal right to use."

"Correct."

"But how did this get you fired?"

Sanna grunted. "Well, Peerage Maker isn't a standalone scam. It's part of this larger corporation, one that appears to be a conglomeration of con games that advertise heavily on YouTube. So-called charities that give one cent of every dollar raised to good works, and the other ninety-nine cents goes into the corrupt pockets of the people running the scam. Ads for kitchenware that breaks on the first usage. Stuff like that. They're con men, but apparently they've become one of the company's biggest customers. And they struggle to stay *just barely* legal. They hire a lot of lawyers– including my former employers – to check the laws to give them safety from prosecution. You know that line from the Cumberbatch *Sherlock*, of course, Addy? In that show, they called Moriarty a "consulting criminal." And that's what's going on with this shady company. People can write to them with ideas for schemes, and if the company decides that it's worth pursuing, they'll fund the ethically dubious project and the person who submitted the idea will get a percentage. It's for people who don't have the money and time to cheat people themselves, but who'd like to make some money from a twisted little idea.

And when I confronted my supervisor about it, I didn't realize that he was on a conference call with a representative from the company who for some reason took umbrage to the fact that I believed that Peerage Maker and their ilk were criminals with a boardroom. There were some heated words from all sides, you don't need me to repeat them, a couple of items from my supervisor's desk may or may not have been thrown, and the long and the short of it is that several minutes later, my supervisor told me that he believed that in the long run everybody would be happier if I decided to pursue other employment opportunities. After a snippy chat with personnel, I cleaned out my cubicle, and lugged two boxes of my possessions with me on the bus on the way back to the flat."

"You might have grounds for a lawsuit," Zabel observed.

"I'm considering it, but right now I'm too steamed to consider anything seriously. "Only sue coldblooded," that's what one of my professors drummed into my head when I was studying law."

"So how does this have anything to do with Lord Hunniraube?" After a moment's consideration, I asked, "Is he even a real lord, or did he just pay Peerage Maker a chunk of cash for a square inch of land?"

Sanna drained half the contents of her water glass. "I thought you'd ask about that. I may be wading into some ethically murky areas here, so I'm going to have to ask you to sleuths to use your deductive skills a bit. Please ask yourselves this question. Where do you think that the land being sold by Peerage Maker is located?"

"On the Hunniraube estate," Zabel and I said simultaneously.

"I can neither confirm nor deny that," Sanna replied, nodding vigorously. "Now this question relies on public knowledge, so I can tell you if you're right or wrong. Besides Jasper, can you think of a YouTube channel that has been frequently sponsored by Peerage Maker over the past few months?"

It took a half-second of thinking before Zabel and I once again replied in near unison, "The Monster Hunterz."

"Correct again," Sanna answered, forgetting that she wasn't supposed to tell us we were right about our guess regarding the first question. "I did a quick search on my phone while I was waiting for our flight. Every last one of their last twelve videos featured a little personalized commercial for Peerage Maker, both at the beginning and at the end. So they were no strangers to Peerage Maker, and they even called themselves "Lord Val" and "Lord Fergie" at one point."

"'P.M.' stands for 'Peerage Maker!'" I exclaimed, immediately realizing I needed to explain my comment to Sanna and Jasper. I told them how those initials appeared in their notes.

"Hmm." Zabel turned to me. "Addy, how many of their videos have you seen?"

"Only two beginning to end. A couple minutes at the beginning of a few others."

"I haven't seen any. I think that we should both take some time after dinner to watch them later, and see if there's something of note–"

She was interrupted by our waitress opening the doors and delivering Jasper and my soup, the beverages, and a basket full of warm Scottish oatmeal rolls with the creamiest, softest butter I'd ever eaten. We all started eating, mulling over everything. Halfway through her roll, Zabel asked Jasper, "Are you going to be in any trouble regarding your connection to Peerage Maker?"

"I don't see why. If Sanna's allegations are indeed true –"

"They are," Sanna informed him.

"Then I'll cut ties with them immediately, post a video about what I've learned, and... if the situation warrants it, then I'm going to be compelled to take all the money that I received from them and donate to a worthy charity." He took a spoonful of soup with a bit too much slurping to be ignored convincingly. "My reputation is based on my being completely honest about everything, from my takes on modern entertainment, to the goods and services I recommend in the advertisements; it's definitely going to hurt my wallet, but what else can I do?"

I smiled in approval. "It sounds like you've got a good grasp of your ethical compass."

"So will you two be prepared to cover my rent money for a few weeks until I get new sponsors?"

Sanna choked. "I'm out of a job. I was going to ask Addy to help me out if I need it."

"Oh." I did a quick mental check of my bank account. "I think I can keep us all housed and fed if need be, at least for a month or two. But is there any chance that somebody might pay us for something at some point?"

"I don't know," Zabel answered. "I was hoping to make a profit with my videos on the case. We're not licensed private enquiry agents. I'm not sure if we can charge any money for investigating. Plus it's not like the police are encouraging our involvement."

After agreeing, I asked Sanna, "You said that you suspected Lord Hunniraube was behind this –"

Before I could finish my thought, she cut in, saying, "Why shouldn't I? It's his land, isn't it?"

"But do you know anything about him?"

"He's a rich aristocrat. A *real* aristocrat. He's probably land rich and cash poor and greedy."

I didn't want to call her out for making false assumptions, but Zabel cut in before I could phrase my comments as tactfully as possible. "If you'd ever met Lord Hunniraube, you'd have serious doubts, as I do, that he's capable of deliberately perpetuating a fraud using his land."

"What do you mean? Is he so honest, pleasant, and upright that you can't possibly see him as a con man?"

"It's more than that," I explained, and while trying to be as respectful of Lord Hunniraube as possible, I described his demeanor and mental state with sufficient thoroughness to paint a full picture of the man and his obsessions.

After a few minutes of explanation, Sanna didn't look as confident as she had a few minutes previously. "Do you promise me you're not having a laugh at my expense?"

"Cross our hearts."

"He could be faking, of course."

"That's a very long con, and there's something in his eyes that no actor could emulate. I genuinely believe he's for real."

I concurred with Zabel. "Plus, I don't think he focuses very much on the funding and day-to-day matters dealing with running the manor. He needs money for buying bait and traps to catch the Loch Ness Monster… which makes me wonder, how does he pay for it? Does he have his own credit card, or does he still have access to all of his accounts? If he's skilled enough at defending himself to stay out of a mental hospital, then he's sharp enough to prevent having control of all of his assets being transferred to one of his relatives. I wonder how the whole budgeting issue at the manor works."

"Come to think of it, I wonder how much money Philly and Lachlan have of their own," Zabel added. "Think about it. Philly's mother passed away, but we don't know how much went to her daughter and how much went to her husband. She probably hasn't inherited very much money, though I could be wrong. Who knows what's happened with her grandparents and any aunts or uncles? And Lachlan, given that he was only the stepson of the previous Lord Hunniraube, he may not have inherited much either. Aristocratic estates are often entailed so that the eldest child – often a son – born of legally married parents gets the lion's share. Of course, his mother may have split her money more equally between her boys, but we don't know how much she had to leave. Anyway, if he's working for his younger half-brother's estate, it's likely he's not that financially independent. So Philly and Lachlan may have only the manor as their main source of income. What if one of them wanted more? Suppose that one of them made a deal with Peerage Maker in order to get some much-needed cash?"

"It's a theory, but that's a lot of assumptions regarding their financial state," Sanna replied. "For all you know those two have mountains of their own money. Of course, being filthy rich never stopped anybody from wanting more."

"Yes, but if Peerage Maker is the obvious scam you describe it as being, then whoever signed up for it would have to know that it would be uncovered sooner or later. That means exposure and embarrassment at the least, and criminal charges and lawsuits at the worst. Why would a titled family risk everything when exposure and a devastating fallout were inevitable? Using your own land for a fraud like that is pretty much just signing your name to a confession."

No one could come up with a response to my points, and we all pondered the situation for a bit once our main course was delivered. Both pies were warm and satisfying, but my favorite part was the melted cheese in the potato pie.

As we finished, Zabel said, "Well, at least now we have a possible motive for the crime. Maybe the Monster Hunterz were looking into the land to check out a shady sponsor, and one of the Hunniraube family decided they had to be silenced?"

"What are you going to do now?" Jasper asked.

"Sanna, I think you need to call the chief constable. Not only did you promise to talk to him when you got here, but you also need to tell him about this possibly pertinent information."

"I know, I know, Addy. I was just too wet and frustrated to talk to a policeman an hour ago. Plus I wanted my dinner. That's another lesson I learned while studying for the bar. Never speak to the authorities when you're hungry. If you enter into conversation with them on an empty stomach, they can hold the prospect of your next meal over you for hours. But now, I can interact with them."

Sanna pulled out her mobile, and after a few minutes of conversation, informed us that the police would be coming to the hotel to speak to us. "He sounded pleasant and not at all hostile, but you never know."

We wrapped up our meal. The pies were particularly filling, so Sanna, Zabel, and I, decided to call it quits, but Jasper ordered enough Dundee cake for all four of us.

"This is a nice little room," Jasper noted, looking around the tiny dining booth. "I'm going to ask them if I can record here tonight. It's soundproof, the acoustics are good. The benches are reasonably comfortable... as long as the Wi-Fi works, I'll get all my equipment and set it up in here." That sounded like a decent plan to me, especially since that meant he wouldn't be commandeering our hotel room for his work.

The waitress thought it would be fine for him to use the room, so Jasper fetched his camera, microphones, and laptop, and the rest of us waited in the lounge for Chief Constable Griogair to arrive. Only a couple of minutes later, he arrived with another police officer we hadn't met yet. Griogair balked at having this conversation in a relatively public place, so after a quick word with the night manager, we were allowed to sit use a cramped office in the back of the hotel.

There's a big difference between being questioned and being interrogated, and this was clearly a case of the former. Not once did I get the sense that Griogair was going to accuse us of killing the Monster Hunterz and stuffing them into the boot of Zabel's car. And his face actually lit up when Sanna started explaining about the whole Peerage Maker situation. His assistant scribbled so fast I thought the pencil was going to catch fire. He asked numerous questions about our experiences here, and we answered willingly.

After about forty minutes, Griogair nodded and rose from a rather rickety-looking wooden chair. "I think that covers everything. Once again, I don't believe that you had anything to do with this, so I believe that everything's properly settled."

"Will you need anything else from us?" Sanna asked.

"Not tonight, but I do think you should give your friends at Hunniraube Manor a call. Miss Phyllida said on multiple occasions that she wanted to talk to you."

"Will it be all right for us to go there tomorrow?"

"Yes, we've finished our search there for now."

"Did you find my clothes?"

"Not yet, Miss Carvalho, but don't give up hope yet." The policemen said their goodnights, and immediately after they left, Zabel called Philly. She answered halfway through the first ring, and it sounded like she had been crying.

"Philly? What's the matter?"

"Can you two please come here first thing in the morning? Maybe at six a.m.?"

"No!"

"Who was that?" Philly asked.

"My name is Sanna Mahabir, I'm their lawyer, and I insist on being present when they speak to you. I'm very tired, I've had a rotten day, and there's no way that I'm getting up before the sun to suit your schedule. We'll be there at nine. No, nine-thirty. Perhaps you could have breakfast ready for us when we get there."

Sounding rather stunned, Philly agreed, and we said we'd see her in the morning.

CHAPTER SEVEN
The Guests Are Fleeing

I definitely was not expecting to sleep well that night. When you realize that you've been riding in a car with a couple of frozen bodies in it, you're justified in assuming that it's going to haunt your nightmares for the next few weeks. I climbed into bed early, expecting disrupted slumber and disrupted visions. What I got was nearly ten hours of uninterrupted rest, and after I washed and dressed myself in a dark green jumper and black trousers, I found myself surprisingly untraumatized and ready for more investigating, even though I knew I wasn't supposed to be playing amateur detective.

I returned a call to Mum, assuring her that Sanna and Jasper had gotten to Inverness safely, and that I hadn't been arrested, and that I definitely had been eating well. After I'd described everything I'd eaten over the last two days down to the last crumb and gotten her approval, she asked if there was anything I needed.

"If you have the time, you can start asking your friends if they know of another job for Sanna. She's going to need a new one." Mum, who hadn't heard the whole story, needed to be filled in, and after becoming properly enraged towards Sanna's former employers for their treatment of her, promised to start making discreet inquiries.

"So, Mum, can you tell me the big secret yet? I'm starting to worry."

"I told you, it's nothing bad. It's something really wonderful, actually, but I just need to wait a bit."

"Do I have a baby brother or sister on the way?"

"Don't be silly, dear."

"And you can't even give a little hint?"

"No. You'll understand when I can tell you, hopefully tomorrow."

And with that, she told me to stay safe, reminded me that she loved me, and told me to give her best to Zabel and Sanna. I wasn't sure why she didn't mention Jasper.

Checking my messages, I saw that Zabel had texted me telling me they were running a little behind, and to meet them downstairs. Halfway down the stairs, I saw a mildly bedraggled Jasper staggering across the hall, carrying a suitcase filled with recording equipment.

"How was your all-night livestream?"

"Profitable. Of course, the hosts were American, so in was more of an all-evening-and-late-to-bed livestream for them, but you get the general idea. We talked about our problems with the recent Marvel shows on Disney+. Over seventy-five thousand viewers total."

"All at once? They all watched the whole thing?"

"Well, no. I don't think anybody does that, except for maybe the mothers of some of the hosts. People drop in and out depending on how much time they have.to spare. Some of our subscribers toss us a few quid or a bit of whatever their home nation's currency is on a regular basis. People have a comment or question they want us to read aloud, so they attach a bit of money to catch our attention. And I'm going to need it, especially if Sanna's right, and I can't keep any of the Peerage Maker money in good conscience. We talked a lot about that tonight. Apparently a bunch of commenters had some particularly salty things to say about the company."

"Really? Do you remember anything interesting?"

"I can't. I'm too tired. But the video has been posted on my YouTube channel. Go ahead and check it out. Right now, I'm crashing. Irn-Bru fueled me through the livestream, but my tank's empty, and I need to snatch a little shut-eye before I start work on my new video on anime news. Have a good day, Addy."

I also wished him well, and as I turned the corner I nearly bumped right into Abhorson.

With his lips curled into his familiar sneer, he said, "Watch yourself. Will you be wanting a table for three or four this morning?"

"Not today, thank you. We'll be having our breakfast elsewhere."

"You'll be missed." The sarcasm was strong with him. Meanwhile, my memory had been working overtime all night, and I finally remembered where I'd seen his face previously.

"Do you know the actor Declan LeCeil?"

The name had a startling effect on him. The sneer vanished as his mouth flew open, the disdain faded from Abhorson's eyes, and the supercilious expression evaporated. He looked almost human now. "How do you know him?"

"Several months ago, when Zabel and I were investigating a robbery at the bank, we realized he might have useful information about a Sherlock Holmes movie for the telly. So we tracked him down to his retirement home, and he very kindly answered our questions. He had a lot of pictures and memorabilia from the plays he'd performed in on his walls, and now I remember, you were in at least one of them." As I looked at Abhorson, I realized his attitude wasn't because he hated the customers. Well, perhaps he didn't like them much, but they weren't the main reason for his surliness. With a sudden flash of comprehension, it became clear that what Abhorson really hated was his *job*. I was quite certain that as a little boy, he hadn't nurtured dreams of becoming a waiter. He'd wanted something much more glamourous out of life, and he was mad at the world for denying him his wish. I put two and two together, and realized that I risked coming up with four billion. "You're an actor, aren't you? You've worked with Declan. Am I right?"

"He was my mentor." Abhorson actually smiled. "I've worked with him on six– no, seven plays since I graduated from RADA, including playing his nephew Ben in *The Sunshine Boys*, and I was Charlie when he played the title character in *Da*. He was always brilliant. You know, we were going to be in a production of *King Lear* a few years ago. Declan was supposed to star, of course, and I was cast as Edmund. It would have been a triumph. Then all the theatres closed, and poor Declan was so crushed by losing out on another opportunity that he decided to retire. And my career took a hit and never recovered. I don't know why, but ever since the stillborn *Lear*, I haven't been able to get a single part. Not one. The last role I ever performed in that made it to a full production was the hairdresser Duane Fox in a revival of the musical *Applause*. It's been years, and once my savings were tapped out, I had to move back to Inverness, and this was the only place that would hire me."

I wouldn't have thought it possible ten minutes earlier, but I actually found myself feeling sorry for Abhorson. I wondered if he acted under his real name, as I'd never heard of a performer with that moniker. Then again, perhaps a slightly different name might be just what was needed to get some much-needed attention in a highly competitive industry. Yet again, perhaps he was so embarrassed about the failure of his acting career that he decided to use an alias for his job as a waiter. I didn't know, and I didn't want to spoil the moment by prying.

Before we had a chance to bond, Zabel and Sanna hurried down the stairs. "Are you ready to go?" Zabel asked.

"Yes." Turning to Abhorson, I told him, "Hope you have a pleasant day."

"You as well, Addy."

The moment we were out the door, Zabel commented, "Wait a minute – did you notice the attitude transplant on him?"

"I did, and I know why." I explained the previous conversation. Sanna needed reminding about who Declan LeCeil was, but Zabel looked impressed.

"Maybe I shouldn't have been so quick to dismiss him as a deeply unpleasant person," she said.

"Don't feel too bad for him yet," Sanna warned her. "You haven't actually seen him act. For all you know, the stage may be a lot better off for having him stuck in a restaurant. Although his personality makes sense to me now. I've worked with plenty of people in the entertainment industry, and I know that they tend to go around the twist if they're denied the opportunity to pursue their creative outlets. You both know that if a certain mustachioed man had been able to make a living painting pictures, he wouldn't have gone into politics and we wouldn't have had to deal with World War Two."

We made our way down the road to the bus stop, reaching it fifteen seconds before the vehicle arrived. Sanna didn't contribute much to the conversation, saying that the hotel bed hadn't treated her well, and she needed a tubful of coffee before she was able to participate in a proper conversation.

Zabel and I mostly made small talk about our theories of the case so far, with Zabel doubting that Lord Hunniraube was really as disturbed as he seemed to be, and I was not so sure that his daughter and half-brother really as nice as they'd been at lunch the previous day.

Zabel tried to convince me that Lord Hunniraube was the likeliest villain of the story, but I wasn't swayed. "Didn't you notice Lord Hunniraube's gait as he walked?" I asked her.'

She cast her mind back, and noted, "He limped a little bit, didn't he?"

"More than a little. Do you recall that Philly mentioned that he had sciatica?"

"I do, now that you mention it."

"He's in his late forties, give or take a bit, and yes, he's powerfully built, but you remember that he has a broken left arm. Whoever put the frozen bodies in your car must have had a lot of upper body strength. I've never tried it myself, but I have serious doubts that a person can lift a human corpse out of a deep freeze with only one arm, let alone transport it even a short distance with sciatic legs. I just don't think he could have done it."

Zabel thought for a moment. "I think you're right. He didn't move the bodies. And with one arm, I don't think he could have put them in the deep freezes in the first place."

"Exactly. So that means that someone else was involved."

"Philly's a petite woman, so I would rule her out as well. So that just leaves Lachlan. Unless you count the staff. And wait a minute... weren't the writers there as well last week? The three we met, they're all sturdy men. They could probably have done the heavy lifting. But why? What possible motive could they have had?"

"That's what I'm wondering, but I think that Lachlan moved the bodies. I don't know if he *killed* them, but I'm pretty sure he's the one who put the corpses in the boot."

"How do you figure that? Because he's got the physical ability to do it, and he was the most likely to have access to that little shed? Which was probably lockable?"

"That's part of it, but do you remember what Lachlan said as he was leaving last night? "I'd suggest you catching a film at the theatre within walking distance down the street, but it's looking like heavy rain is coming, and you don't want to catch a cold after getting drenched.""

"I can't say that I remember that word for word, but that sounds about right."

"Do you notice anything odd about that?"

"It sounds pretty ordinary to me. If it rains, you get wet. Sometimes you even get sick if it's too cold and you're too soaked. That's how it works. Storms soak you, especially when..." A light flashed in her eyes. "You... don't... have... an... umbrella. Because my umbrella was stolen from the car. But we didn't mention that to him. So how did he know? Unless, of course, he was the one who took my clothes and the umbrella from the boot. He gave himself away."

"That's weak, you two," Sanna chastised us. "On a windy day, you can get soaked even with an umbrella. A hat and coat aren't enough to protect you, either. I think you're jumping to conclusions here. There's no definite proof he was implying that you don't have an umbrella, and even less that he took it. And anyway, he knew that you didn't have a car anymore, so you'd be out in the open longer, walking or waiting for the bus. That's not enough to point a finger of accusation."

She had a point. As much as I dislike admitting it, I'm not actually Sherlock Holmes. I just answer his mail.

I was mulling over the very real possibility that I might have to reevaluate my theories when the bus rolled up to our stop, which was a brief walk down the road from Hunniraube Manor. As we strolled along the path, we noticed that there was a caravan of cars heading in the opposite direction. From the expressions on the faces of the people driving, they weren't just going out for a bit of sightseeing for the day. There were suitcases visible in back seats. These were people who had attended the mystery writing conference, and after getting freaked out by a pair of actual murders, were now fleeing, quite possibly out of fear that they'd be the killer's next targets.

As we approached the manor, we saw Lord Hunniraube standing at what appeared to be a turntable. I knew that the man had some problems, but I didn't realize that it had progressed to the point where he had decided to become a disc jockey.

Upon further inspection, I could see that there were electrical cords running from the music equipment into the loch.

"What is that kilt-wearing man doing?" Sanna asked in what she thought was a whisper, but was actually what the average person would consider quite strident. Luckily, Lord Hunniraube couldn't seem to hear her with headphones over his ears. He must have had the volume turned up all the way.

"That's Lord Hunniraube. It appears that he's playing music over underwater speakers in the hopes that it will attract the Loch Ness Monster to emerge. Or maybe it's not meant to attract Nessie so much as cause so much annoyance that it will rise up to the surface in order to get away from the racket. I'm not sure what his strategy is."

"I take it we shouldn't approach him?"

"That would probably be best."

Waldroup met us in front of the main doors, just as a grim-faced couple pushed past him, hauling their luggage behind them.

"How many people are leaving?" I asked.

"All the guests, and all of the mystery writers except for three. McLennan, Ginnungagap, and Ícidhe. Have you met them?"

"Yes, we have. At least, Zabel and I did. Sanna hasn't. But why are they staying when… wait a minute. They were here a week ago, weren't they? When the Monster Hunterz were killed. So they might be suspects, but if the other writers and the guests came *afterwards*, then they're in the clear and the police wouldn't need them to stick around, and judging from the looks on their faces, they'd read enough mysteries to know that it's not the smartest idea to stay in a hotel where there's a killer on the loose."

"Philly had to refund everybody's money, and now people who are registered for upcoming conferences here are cancelling en masse."

"Is she all right?" Zabel asked.

"No. She's... not at her best right now. She's..."

We had been walking and talking, and we were now in the main hall. An off-key rendition of "Shang-A-Lang" was reverberating throughout the room, and as my eyes darted around, trying to find the source of the tuneless sound, I discovered Philly sprawled out in a plush chair in one corner, with a decanter on the floor next to her and a glass in her hand. As I approached her, I was met by the scent of whisky.

"Does she usually day drink?" Zabel whispered to Waldroup.

"Only when her father's really acting up, and even then, I've never known her to have more than a sip or two."

"Shang-A-Lang" was finally finished, and Philly looked at us with eyes that acknowledged our presence without really looking at us. "I'm a failure," she slurred. "I'm a flop at running a conference centre."

"And you haven't got the pipes for a singing career either," said Sanna with her usual delicacy.

Philly filled her glass up to the brim, and with a "no, no, no," Zabel ran forward, plucked the decanter from Philly's hand, and wrested away with glass without much difficulty, though a good slosh of whisky splashed over her hand. Philly objected, but she was in no condition to fight back. After Zabel set the glass and decanter off to the side, I offered her my handkerchief, which she accepted with a smile.

The scent of cheap body spray mingled with the whisky fumes, and as I turned around, I saw that Gavin Ginnungagap had wandered into the hall, and was now leaning over Philly. "The lady's had a bit too much to drink. I'll help her to her room and she can have a lie-down."

The leer on his face gave all of us chills, and we knew at once that wasn't a good idea. "She's my girlfriend. I'll help her." Waldroup hurried forward, scooped up Philly, and hurried away. Ginnungagap shrugged, shot Zabel a smile that made me apprehensive, and slinked away.

"Who the hell was that lech?" Sanna asked. We brought her up to speed, and she snorted. "Remind me never to buy one of his books."

"Zabel? Addy?" We turned to see Lachlan, his arms full of assorted papers. "I'm glad you came. I'd like to have a word with you, but I'm afraid I have my plate filled to the ceiling right now. You haven't had breakfast yet, have you?"

"No. We were expecting to eat here."

"That's excellent, actually. Why don't you head to the dining room? We've got all this food on the buffet, as we were expecting all of the guests to eat, but they didn't want to touch our food. I think they're worried that it's poisoned. It's not," he added with just enough haste to make us suspicious.

"Is there coffee?" Sanna inquired.

"Pots of it."

"Brilliant." Sanna led the way down the corridor. There weren't any signs, but we were able to follow our noses, as the smell of coffee and smoked fish were almost overpowering.

There were only two other people in the dining room, Stetson and Cian. Stetson rose as he saw us, and Cian followed awkwardly a moment later.

"Morning, Zabel! Addy! Good to see y'all again. And who is this?"

After we'd introduced Sanna, Stetson encouraged us to help ourselves to the buffet while everything was still warm. Under the chafing dishes, there were scrambled eggs with smoked salmon, kedgeree with haddock, Scottish morning rolls with butter, and a bowl labelled "Highland Applesauce." I wasn't sure why it had that name until I took a sniff and realized it was full of whisky. Perhaps that had formed the basis of Philly's breakfast. I helped myself to generous portions of everything else, and joined the others at the table. Sanna downed two cups of coffee before leaving the buffet, and managed to carry two more cups back to the table, all while also holding a well-filled plate.

"It's good that you've come to help us prevent this spread from going to waste," Cian commented. "The guests are fleeing, and the staff are giving their notices."

"I'm glad the kitchen staff stuck around long enough to prepare this breakfast," Sanna responded. "This coffee is made just the way I like it. Super strong."

"Are they able to leave now? I thought they were under suspicion."

Cian nodded in response to my question. "They have to stay on the premises, or at least in the general area, until this case is resolved, but once they're done, they're out of here."

"If they catch the killer, then the danger's gone," I reasoned. "Why would they need to leave?"

"Apparently, they're all sick of having to deal with Lord Hunniraube and his... eccentricities."

"Ah, yes. I forgot."

Stetson buttered the remaining half of his morning roll. "So, are you two investigating us?"

I knew that my knee-jerk response of "Why would you think that?" was pretty disingenuous, and I felt myself squirm after saying it. Fortunately, Stetson and Cian both laughed as if my attempt at dissembling were the funniest thing they'd ever seen.

"Relax, buddy," Stetson chuckled. "We're crime writers. We both know that if you're not suspecting everybody, you're not doing your job."

"But it's not his job," Sanna countered. "He earns his paycheck by writing letters to the desperate and delusional. You've got a multiple murderer who has no compunction about using your vehicle as a dumping ground for corpses. Don't get me wrong—" she spread out her hands, sloshing a bit of coffee on the carpet as she did so. "You did a pretty good job digging up the truth of that bank robbery several months ago, but I'm really suspecting that you're starting to push your luck."

Stetson and Cian looked at each other. "Well, now we're embarrassed to tell you what we've been up to lately," Stetson told us.

"What do you mean?" As soon as I asked, I knew. "You've started your own investigation, haven't you?"

"It's an occupational hazard for mystery writers," Cian replied with a slightly embarrassed expression. "We spend so much time crafting twisty plots and crafting clever clues, sooner or later we all start to wonder how good we'd be at solving a real-life crime."

I nodded. "That's true. Sir Arthur Conan Doyle got involved in multiple investigations where he played a pivotal role in clearing the names of two wrongly convicted men. In the George Edalji case, where he was charged with attacking animals…" I stopped, as I could tell that no one at the table was particularly interested in what I had to say. The case at hand was more important, and Cian and Stetson clearly wanted to talk about their attempts to become detectives, and Zabel and Sanna were interested in hearing what they had to say. I mumbled briefly about how I was digressing, and turned back to my scrambled eggs, making it clear that I was finished talking for the moment.

"Well, I learned a long time ago that successful fiction is all about wish fulfillment," Stetson explained. "That's what my books are all about. Non-stop excitement and actions where the good guys win over the villains, and the men meet incredible women and find love. That's what people want from their lives, and I give it to them, and I make plenty of money. Ordinary people live quiet, monotonous existences, and they'll jump at the chance to live vicariously at an action hero's existence. But what a lot of laypeople don't realize is us, Jessica Fletcher on *Murder, She Wrote* and Richard Castle on *Castle* are living the dream. It doesn't matter how high you are on the bestseller list; mystery writers want a little bit more out of life. So-called "literary" writers are always salivating over the next big industry prize, the one that they think will assure their reputations and immortality. Thriller writers know that they're never going to get that kind of respect from the critical snobs, so they want something else. They want to become their characters, and they want to try their own mettle as a detective. Wouldn't it be nice to catch murderers yourself? And it's not just a selfish motive. You want to do some good for society." He pointed his coffee spoon towards me. "You understand, don't you, Addy? You've been a Sherlock Holmes fan all your life, and how did you feel when you finally got the chance to live your literary idol's life?"

"Amazing." Abruptly realizing that I was a bit too enthusiastic, I quickly amended that statement, dissembling with a hasty, "Of course, it was terrible that an actual human being died, I didn't take any pleasure from that."

"Of course you didn't. But you *did* enjoy unravelling the truth, and you can't blame Cian and I for wanting a bite of the apple ourselves, can you?"

Cian flicked a grain of rice off of the sleeve of his leather jacket. I wasn't quite sure why he was wearing it indoors, incidentally. The central heating was turned up rather high, and it was a bit too warm for my tastes. "This is the first time I've ever had the chance of solving a real-life case."

"I think you two will make for a great sleuthing team. How much investigation have you done so far?" Zabel asked. "You must be way ahead of us, as you've been so much closer to the action than we have." She was deliberately flattering them, but only someone who knew Zabel pretty well would have noticed that she was gripping her left wrist with her right hand, one of her little tells that gives away when she's being insincere. I often see her doing that when she's trying to coax information out of a recalcitrant witness. The last time she held her own wrist when talking to me was a couple of months ago, when I wore a pink and gold-striped tie my sister-in-law gave me, and she told me that I looked stylish. I have never worn that tie since.

"Well, we've figured out that the perpetrator needed to be around at the time of the crime, so that rules out all of the guests and most of the writers who are here as speakers. That just leaves the owners and staff, and those few writers who were on hand early enough to be here when the Monster Hunterz disappeared," Cian explained.

"And we know we didn't do it." Stetson spoke calmly and without a hint of defensiveness. "So that leads us to our chief suspect: Gavin Ginnungagap."

"What exactly put him at the top of your 'most likely murderer' list?" Sanna asked.

"Well for starters, have you *seen* him?"

Sanna reflected on Stetson's question for a minute. "You're right. He's clearly guilty of something. Though I would have gone with some sort of sexually based offence."

"I admit that guy gives me the chills," Zabel concurred, "but what exactly do you think his motive was for killing them?"

"Ah, yes," Cian said. "There's the rub. You see, we're coming up empty there."

"We've done some digging online, and we have no idea why Gavin would have anything against the two of them. No evidence to suggest anything untoward, or any financial motive as well."

"Do you know anything about Peerage Maker?" Sanna asked?

"Never heard of it," Cian replied.

Stetson stroked his chin. "Peerage Maker… I've seen that on a bunch of YouTube videos I've watched lately. Doesn't it claim to give someone an aristocratic title if they send in a check?"

"More or less, yes."

"Not for me. We don't go in for those sorts of things where I come from. Plain 'Mister McLennan' is good enough for me."

"And being Irish," Cian added, "you can probably deduce how I feel about the British titled aristocracy."

"Are either of you connected to a YouTube channel?" Zabel asked.

Both shook their heads. "I have a bunch of fans who talk about my work, and the studios producing the Ted Testosterone thriller movies put the trailers on there, but for the most part I stay off the Internet and avoid the plague of social media in all its forms. If I need to self-promote my books and the adaptations, I have an assistant to handle that."

"And niche playwrights and crime show creators don't get that much attention. Nothing ruins a writer like excessive ease in voicing his opinions to the world. It used to be that a man with a message had to spend hours carefully honing his arguments, harnessing all of his talent for wielding the written word, polishing his work into the most impressive diatribe possible, and then fighting tooth and nail with an editor to print it, before having to wait who knows how long for it to reach the public, and even longer for a reply. Now, you can spew your venom in seconds and send it out to billions of people without even having to proofread. It's the death of many a thoughtful scribbler."

Zabel nodded and pressed forward. "Had either of you ever heard of the Monster Hunterz before?"

They replied in the negative. "Which makes us wonder, what if those two weren't killed for their connection to the killer, but because they just happened to be in the wrong place at the wrong time?"

"What do you mean?"

"Well, look at our man Gavin," Cian explained. "He's the sort of man you never under any circumstances would allow to work at a daycare centre."

Feeling the morning rolls weighing down my stomach, I looked around with more than a little trepidation. "He might hear you."

"I rather doubt that," Cian shrugged. "He had one bun and a cup of tea for breakfast, and announced that since his morning lecture had been cancelled, and since the police are letting us leave the property as long as we stay in Inverness, that he was going to do a little sightseeing and pay a visit to Aleister's place."

"Is this Aleister a friend of his?" Sanna asked.

"No, he's long dead. I'm referring to Aleister Crowley. You know of him?"

Sanna didn't, Zabel had heard the name but couldn't place it at the moment. "He was a famous writer during the first half of the twentieth century," I explained, "with a reputation for being 'the wickedest man in the world.' He had an interest in diabolism and tried to start his own new religion, stressing the occult. His drug use and sex life scandalized society, and he was involved in a lot of shady stuff."

"Exactly," Cian nodded. "So, Crowley's finances ebbed and flowed over the course of his life. At one point, he was able to afford Boleskine House, a manor on Loch Ness's shore, not too far from here. Over the centuries, there were stories about magical rituals and necromancy being performed there. No idea how embellished those tales were, but that's why Crowley was interested in the place. Long after Crowley died, Jimmy Page of Led Zeppelin owned it for a while. During the 2010s, the place was wiped out by a pair of fires four years apart. The current owners are trying to rebuild it, but they've had to deal with occultists who have been trespassing on the property."

"And Gavin," Stetson informed us as he scraped the last flakes of salmon from his plate, "has an interest in the occult."

"I didn't know that," I said.

"Haven't you heard about the controversy behind his last couple of books? Aside from all of the explicit sex stuff, some of the… activity was connected to some demonic rituals." Stetson shook his head. "In America, we have the First Amendment, and when some folks wanted to ban Gavin's books at my local library, I spoke out against censorship. But as a parent, I believe I have a personal duty to prevent my young children from reading that smut."

"Gavin's not one of the authors where I keep myself informed about his career," I explained.

"Can't blame you."

"But it seems to me likely," Cian said. "Given Gavin's reputation for getting into all sorts of shocking behaviour, that the Monster Hunterz might have seen, and then in order to keep them quiet he –"

"Look, you may not be my clients, but if you want to stay out of the courtroom, I suggest that you leave that right there," Sanna said, swallowing her kedgeree. "Theorizing about someone's carnal life and hypothesizing that he may be a murderer is a remarkably effective way of getting yourself hauled into court on a slander lawsuit. Of course, in this case, the judge would take one look at Gavin and immediately rule in your favor, but it's still not smart to suggest that a man in the public eye was caught having a go at it with the Loch Ness Monster and then murdered two men to shut them up." I thought to myself that given her past comments, Sanna should take her own advice, but I said nothing.

"Besides," Zabel added, "from what I've heard about Gavin, he's pretty open about everything he gets up to. I just don't think he'd care enough to kill in order to keep his activities quiet. If anything, he'd enjoy the publicity. I just don't see a motive there."

Cian and Stetson looked disappointed by Zabel's reasoning, and they had no reply to her rebuttal.

"Well he could have –"

"What did I just say about theorizing?" Sanna had brought the coffee carafe to the table, and she helped herself to another cup.

After a moment's silence, Stetson asked without any malice, "Do you have any more questions for us?"

"What do you mean?"

"Well, Cian and I have ruled ourselves out because we know that we didn't do it. But I know we're still on your list of suspects."

Zabel wasn't clutching her own wrist, but besides that, I could tell by the light in her eyes that she was being completely sincere. "We don't want it to be either of you two. We like you."

"Well, thank you, Miss Zabel, and I'd like to return the complement. But you know how mysteries work. You have to suspect everybody, no matter how fond you are of them. It's your duty as an amateur detective."

"Thanks for your understanding."

"It's all part of the crime writer code. You can't teach people to consider everybody who pops up in your books to be a potential murder, and then get indignant when, after two fellows wind up dead a stone's throw away from you, people wonder if you might be involved."

"What possible motive might you have?" I asked.

"Beats me."

"I can't think of any reason why I would have been involved in their deaths."

"Besides," Stetson explained, "We have alibis for the night those two disappeared."

"Oh?"

"Yes, we both had nighttime seminars after dinner – this is with the last group of people who attended, not the ones who just left. Then we were both cornered by people and talking until nearly midnight. That's the thing. The gates at the manor close around ten, so we wouldn't have been able to drive our cars off the property. The buses around here stop service well before midnight, and as I told the police, you can check with every cab driver in Inverness, none of them picked us up that night. There's no way either of us could left the grounds, met the Monster Hunterz in town, killed them, and lugged their bodies back here."

"You know, I've been wondering about that," I said.

"Wondering about our alibis?"

"No. The Monster Hunterz were last seen some distance from here, drinking at some pubs. If they were killed that night, then they must have been brought back to Hunniraube Manor, either dead or alive. So why were they taken here, when they might have been discovered at any point and the corpses would have linked the crime directly with the manor?"

Everybody thought for a minute. "Maybe the killer knew there was a place on the property where no one else would ever look." Zabel mused. "Which points in the direction of the family."

"Maybe," Cian agreed, "but to double back, we both have alibis until well after one in the morning as well."

"I was on a Zoom call with my family back in Texas from midnight to one-thirty."

"And I was on the phone with my agent in New York City from twelve-fifteen to a bit past one, discussing *The Castrator of Sevenmilelane*."

"Wait, what?" The three of us spoke in unison.

"You know how my niche has always been writing parodies of other playwrights' work? Usually in mystery form?"

"Yes." I suddenly realized who was the target of his latest satire. "You're riffing on Martin McDonagh now."

"Exactly. You know that his plays are famous for portraying dysfunction in small, backwards Irish towns. They're all about hostile relationships, anger, and thy usually involve some sort of maiming. So my latest play riffs on all of that. It's set in a fictional village on an island just off the west coast of Ireland, and it's such a wretched place that someone has decided that the community needs to fade out of existence, so one of the villagers – everybody suggests a particularly poorly treated woman – begins a campaign of castration against the hard-drinking men of Sevenmilelane. It's a mystery, and the villagers have to catch the perpetrator before every man in the village loses his manhood. What do you think?"

"You had me at 'castrator,' Sanna replied.

"It certainly sounds like something McDonagh would write. I wouldn't suggest it to couples on their first date, though," said Zabel.

I answered with something positive sounding and non-committal. I wasn't thinking of the play so much as the fact that the alibis only worked if the Monster Hunterz were actually killed on the night they disappeared. But what if they hadn't died that night? What if they'd simply left town to investigate something, and when they returned a day or two later, they were killed then? That possibility meant that we couldn't be sure of their innocence.

"Thanks! I've been snacking on Kimberley biscuits and Tayto crisps to get into the right mindset as I write. I'm glad I'm finished with the draft. I've put on six pounds since I started writing this blasted play."

Zabel was about one syllable into a response when both Cian and Stetson's mobiles chimed. "It's a text from Gavin," a confused-looking Stetson informed us. "He wants us to meet him at Boleskine House in one hour. He says he's uncovered the reason why the Monster Hunterz were killed."

CHAPTER EIGHT
The Great Sausage Scandal

"Addy, are you all right? You look upset."

Shaking my head, I told Zabel, "I feel fine. I'm just thinking. Particularly, about the bodies being found in your car."

By this point, we had finished our breakfast, and we were now heading out to Boleskine House. As all of us were familiar with standard mystery tropes, and none of us had any particular reason to trust Gavin, we were all suspicious of some sort of trap, especially since Gavin had sent Stetson and Cian another text, warning them not to share this information with the police, though he provided no reasons as to why they shouldn't.

"Before we leave, can take a look over here. I want to take a look at where we were parked yesterday."

Everybody agreed, looking curious at my suggestion. We walked through the garden, past the statue of Lord Hunniraube with his turtle, and then along a paved walkway. "As far as I can tell, this is the closest and most direct route from the manor to the shed and the little car park where we were yesterday." After a few seconds, the pen where Kratos the guard dog was held became visible. "All of you wait here, please. I'll be back in two minutes." No one objected, and I walked past Kratos, and then followed the path down the to shed we'd parked next to, the one which had presumably held the bodies. The area had been cordoned off with police tape, and then I walked back to the others.

"Please, humour me. This is an experiment that may help us. Zabel, would you please follow the path down to the shed and come back?" She did, and two minutes later she returned with an arched eyebrow.

"Did you see something there that I didn't?" she asked.

"No. And it's not about seeing." I turned to the others. "I really appreciate your patience with this. Sanna, will you go next, please?" She did, and when she came back, her face was tolerant, but her expression made it clear that whatever I was building up towards had better be worth it. "Now you, please, Stetson." He started down the path, but as soon as he came within three yards of the pen, Kratos started barking madly.

"I don't think that dog likes me," he shouted back to us.

"Actually, I rather doubt that he has a problem with you. Come back, please. You don't have to go any further." As Stetson headed back towards us, Kratos's barks turned to mournful howls, which gradually faded away once he got closer to us.

"This is confirming my suspicions," I said.

"Towards me?" a surprised-looking Stetson asked.

"Oh, no. Please excuse me. That's not what I meant. Give me another minute, and I'll be able to explain. Cian, will you please do exactly what the others did?"

He did, and when he was approximately the same distance from the pen as Stetson was, Kratos started barking again. "He does that every time I walk by," Cian informed us.

"Yes, and I think he has his reasons for it, which have nothing to do with you. Please come back."

"What do you mean?" Cian asked, as the barking turned to plaintive howling and then faded away altogether.

"Do you remember when we spoke yesterday? You told us that he was a barker, but he stopped if you gave him a treat."

"That's true." Cian slapped himself on the forehead. "It's not me, it's the food! I grew up with lots of big, hungry dogs. Mostly black labs. They're very food-oriented. I suppose Rottweilers are the same way."

"But you were holding a ham sandwich then," Zabel reminded us.

"Well, ham and cheese, but your point is valid," Cian agreed. "I'm not carrying food now, but I often carry a snack while taking a walk. I know, I know. It cancels out some of the benefits of the exercise, but I just get hungry.

"Right…" I took a deep breath, and the scent of leather gave me an idea. "Cian, please take off your jacket and do the walk again. I'll hold it for you. You can borrow my coat if you're chilly."

"I'll be fine," Cian assured me, handing me his leather jacket. I took the opportunity to examine it. It appeared to be of good quality, but it had a strong odor of tanned leather. When Cian reached Kratos, the dog was silent.

After he returned, I made the trip down to the pen with his jacket draped over my arm, and Kratos went wild again. After I returned and I handed Cian back his jacket, Stetson was on the same page I was. "My Buc-ees jerky." He pulled a bag out of his coat pocket, then another out of a different coat pocket, and then a third bag of jerky out of his blazer pocket. He handed them to me, and then made it to Kratos without provoking a round of eardrum-shattering barking.

"It's the scent of meat or leather – I noticed the rawhide toys in his pen – that sets him off!" Stetson said as he took back his jerky. "I think that dog deserves a little treat. Not the ghost pepper or the garlic beef jerky. The spices might not sit well with him. He might like the cherry maple, though." Stetson pulled a little handful of jerky out of one bag, jogged down to the pen, and tossed it over to Kratos, who gave a delighted series of yips before scarfing down the dried meat.

After Stetson hurried back, Cian noted, "All right. Now we know that the dog will bark like crazy when there's some sort of animal product he wants to devour or at least chew on. We didn't realize this until now, which means that if either of us had walked along that route to the shed to put the bodies in your car, then the dog would have made a lot of noise.

"And when we were here yesterday, the only time we heard Kratos barking was when Cian came by with his ham and cheese sandwich." Zabel paused for a moment. "And his jacket."

"I feel like I should point out that it's possible that someone could have taken a longer route, one that avoids the dog pen," Sanna, ever willing to throw cold water on my theories, noted.

"You'd have to go all the way around that road, and then hike through those thick woods," Zabel argued. "It would take four times as long, and the person would've been in a hurry, because he – I'm just going to use the masculine pronoun here for convenience – knew the job would take some time, and someone else could have wandered by at any moment. Besides, the point is that we didn't hear the dog barking."

"Exactly! It's straight out of 'Silver Blaze.'"

"What's that, now?" Sanna asked.

"'Silver Blaze' is a Sherlock Holmes short story. It's the one where he notes that the vital clue was 'the curious incident of the dog in the night-time' – that's where the Mark Haddon novel got its title. The dog did nothing in the night-time. That was the curious incident. Kratos didn't bark. I know it's not proof positive, but Cian's jacket and Stetson's jerky give them alibis. At least, something alibi-ish."

We were quiet for a few moments, and then Cian informed us, "Gavin's a vegan, incidentally."

I mulled over that point for a moment. "Thanks for mentioning that. I don't know if that will mean anything one way or another, but it's something to consider. I reiterate that Cian's jacket has a strong leather smell. Most shoes and belts don't have the same odor, so they don't set off the dog's nose."

Stetson chuckled. "So my jerky habit wound up clearing my name with an odd kind of alibi. Take that, my cardiologist." He helped himself to another handful of jerky.

"I wonder –" I stopped, as Lachlan appeared from behind a clump of trees and headed towards us. He looked frazzled, and I decided to ask him some tactful, subtle questions as a means of getting some information from him. Other members of my group, however, had different ideas.

Stetson went straight to the point. "Hey! Lachlan! How many people had keys to that shed? The one with the freezers?"

After a gulp, Lachlan answered, "I have one, and my half-brother has one as well. Two of the groundskeepers have keys also. But that doesn't mean anything. I'm always losing my keys, and since nothing of value is in there, I keep a key to the shed in a little magnetic box hidden under that bit of the roof of to the side."

"Have you told many people about it?"

"No, none at all, but as I told the police, someone could have hidden in the woods somewhere and seen me. I used it a couple of times over the past week, so it's possible that I was watched."

"Skillful job shifting suspicion to some unknown person," Sanna muttered at a volume that she *thought* was under her breath.

Lachlan, whose ears were clearly in fine working order, stiffened his posture and defensiveness entered his voice. "Is that meant to be an accusation? Do you believe that I broke into that car, took out Miss Zabel's clothes and umbrella, and then stuffed a pair of frozen corpses in there?"

"Well, *now* I think that," Zabel said. There was a level of ferocity in her voice that I'd rarely seen previously.

"What... what do you mean?"

"I was talking about this earlier. Last night, you talked about it being a good thing that we weren't going out, as we could get very wet. I'd only mentioned my missing clothes that were taken from the boot. We never said anything about the umbrella. You implied that I didn't have an umbrella anymore last night, but you were vague enough that I couldn't take that as a definite admission of guilt. But now, you explicitly mentioned the umbrella, something you couldn't have known about unless you were the one who stole my possessions and ruined my car!"

Lachlan crumbled. He started shaking and blubbered a bit, and eventually staggered off to one side and sank down upon a very uncomfortable-looking stone bench. After a few moments he looked up at us with anxious eyes. "Please don't ask me to replace your car. I can't afford it."

"*That's* what you're concerned about?" I responded in what I realized too late was a bellow. "Paying for a new car is what worries you? Not the legal fallout of depositing two dead bodies in a near-stranger's vehicle?"

"But I didn't kill them! I just needed to get the bodies off the estate before one of the groundskeepers wandered in and found them!"

"If you aren't the murderer, who is?" Zabel asked.

"My half-brother, of course! We all knew he was mad, but I never realized just how dangerous he really was until I went into that shed looking for a coil of rope for tying back a bit of fence that's been shaking in the wind. I lifted up the lid of one of the deep freezes, wondering what sort of bait my brother's been wasting his money on lately, and I saw… and then I looked in the other one…"

"When was this?"

"The morning you came here. I was terrified, because I knew that if the bodies were discovered, the scandal would destroy us. No respectable person wants to stay in a murder hotel. When I saw you parked there, it was like kismet. I couldn't leave the hotel myself, if I was gone for too long, everything here would devolve into chaos. So I knew there was only car on the premises that would be leaving shortly. I didn't think clearly, I know that. All I could see was the possibility of getting the bodies away from here. I panicked. Your car was right by the shed, and no one was around, so I transferred the two corpses into the car."

"I was surprised you told the police about the deep freezes in the shed," I told him.

"I didn't think I had a choice. If they'd discovered them and I hadn't mentioned them, it would've been suspicious. I had to act as if I didn't know for certain that anything was wrong."

"What did you do with my clothes and umbrella?" Zabel asked.

"There's a closet in the basement that's covered up by some paneling. I tucked them inside and pushed some heavy cardboard boxes in front of it. No one would know it was there unless they were looking very closely."

"And then you sent a note to the police? Why? Why not just wait for us to discover the bodies on our own?"

Lachlan shrugged in response to my question. "I told you, I was panicking. I worried that you'd come back to the manor and open up the boot, and then I'd be back where I started, with a murder investigation scaring away the guests. When I saw that blind fellow around looking for an odd job, I quickly wrote out a note, gave him a bit of cash, and told him to take the bus back into town and drop it off at the police station and leave before they could ask questions."

"Did you alter your voice when you spoke to him?" Zabel asked.

"Yes. I adopted an Irish accent. Nothing against Cian, I wasn't trying to incriminate him, but I'd spoken to him earlier and his brogue was on my mind." After a mirthless chuckle, he admitted, "All that trouble and I wound up exactly where I didn't want to be anyway."

None of us were sympathetic towards him. "You still claim you had nothing to do with their deaths?" Zabel asked.

"I swear it!"

"But you had no scruples against putting two dead bodies in my car?"

His face started to turn a rather attractive shade of fuchsia. "Will you get over yourself? You can always get a new car, but if this lodge folds, I lose everything! It's mortgaged up to the hilt, because all of the income from the Hunniraube family fortune went to my half-brother, and he spends everything on his mad quest to hunt the Loch Ness Monster! My only income is a percentage of the profits from the lodge, and most months that's just a bit above nothing. I have no savings, no university education, and no job opportunities if this place closes, unless I wrangle a position as a bellhop at some hotel. I was raised in my little half-brother's shadow. My mother's first marriage was for love. She wanted to go on the stage, and she eloped with one of her colleagues. They were happy, but they were poor teenagers, and shortly after I came around, she decided she couldn't take the tiny attic flats and bit parts in lousy plays, so she crawled back to my grandparents on her knees, and my grandparents arranged for an annulment and set her up with the previous Lord Hunniraube, who had enough scandals in his own past not to care about her linking her lot to a third-rate thespian. I should have gotten a proper share of my maternal grandparents' fortune, but instead my brother got a double portion. The Hunniraubes weren't going to give any money to a stepchild, and my blood grandparents never even looked me in the eye. The only job I've ever had and am ever likely to have is working for my half-brother. I've kept him out of trouble as best I could after he's started spiraling further afield. I literally am my brother's keeper. If he gets locked away and the lodge fails and the bank takes it, I'm homeless and broke. So don't you dare blame me for acting in self-preservation for stuffing those bodies into the boot of your car!"

He stared at us with burning defiance for a few moments, but I wasn't looking at him anymore. I was looking at the police officer who had quietly wandered into the area, and who had overheard his admittance of guilt.

One by one, the others noticed the policeman's presence. I think I just made that sound like it took longer than it really did. It was only three seconds before all of my colleagues saw the newcomer, and a moment later Lachlan swiveled around. The blood drained from his face. He sprang up from the bench, presumably with the misguided idea of sprinting away, but simultaneously, Sanna and Stetson both put a hand on one of his shoulders and pushed him back down onto the bench.

I don't think I need to go into details about the next several minutes of conversation. Anybody who's ever seen an episode of any UK police procedural will have a pretty good idea of what the ensuing dialogue was like. The police officer looked as if he was on his last day before retirement, and he didn't appreciate having to do any actual work during his last few hours of employment.

Frustratingly, the officer seemed to be a lot more upset with us for our amateur sleuthing that he was with Lachlan for moving frozen bodies into a near-stranger's car. He chastised us, and Sanna, who is not one for taking criticism with a smile, pointed out with characteristic directness that he could parlay our deductions into a career boost for himself if he played his cards shrewdly, which shut his mouth nice and tight.

As he led Lachlan away, the police officer managed to get one final gibe in, informing us that, "You're free to go about your business. I just want you to know that I think the chief constable's been much too lenient with you." He directed these words directly to me and Zabel. "If it were up to me, you two would've be in custody until we figured out exactly how those bodies got in your car. He must like you, if he's treating you so leniently."

"What can we say? We can be very charming." Zabel shot the policeman one of her more breathtaking smiles, and he clearly wasn't immune to her charisma. He managed to make an expression that could be called a grin if you wanted to be incredibly charitable. Lachlan staggered along, as if he weren't sure if he was in some sort of nightmare or if this really was happening to him.

We were silent for a moment and then Zabel fished her mobile out of her purse. "I should give Philly a call. She should know what's happened to her uncle." A moment later, she said, "Oh, Waldroup? Do you have Philly's phone? Oh, I see. No, let her rest. But you should be prepared for some shocking news, and perhaps it's better you tell her than the police. Her uncle's the one who put the bodies of the Monster Hunterz in the boot of my car. No, I'm sure. He confessed in front of all of us. To protect the manor from scandal, I guess. I'm not sure if he actually killed them or not. I don't think he did. What? Oh yes, of course. I'll tell you more later." As she ran her finger across the screen of her phone, she explained, "Philly's taken a sedative and now she's resting. The police just showed up and they want to have a word with Waldroup."

"They'll probably want to speak to us again soon," I noted.

"Then perhaps we'd better leave right away," Stetson noted. "If we leave right now, we can make it to Boleskine House just about an hour after Gavin sent us his text."

We followed a different path down to another car park, and Stetson led us to a seven-seat Range Rover. "When I rented this, the clerk told me that this was the same kind of vehicle Queen Elizabeth used to drive. I don't know about that, but I do enjoy driving it, and I know my cars."

"What do you drive back in Texas?" I asked as we climbed inside the Range Rover.

"I've got a garage full of classic cars. My newest acquisition is an Amphicar. Ever hear of that?" None of us had. "It's a car that doesn't just drive on roads. You can take it into water and it'll float above the surface and you can drive across a lake. President Lyndon Baines Johnson had one and loved it. One of his chief sources of amusement was taking guests for a ride in it, and then abruptly pretending that he'd lost control and then racing straight into the lake at his ranch. Then, when the guests were panicking, thinking they were going to drown, he'd start laughing and they'd realize that the car wasn't sinking."

"Do you do that with your guests?" Zabel asked.

"Oh, certainly not. LBJ and I have very different ideas of what we consider funny. I don't like scaring people. But it *is* a fun car to drive. It's a shame the novelty never caught on with the general public."

My mobile rang, and I saw that it was Jasper. "Addy! Thank goodness I got through to you. How soon before you get back here?"

"We're just five or six minutes away. What's the problem?"

"I think I may have stumbled on something important. It's connected with this place called Boleskine House. Ever heard of it?"

"Yes. We just happen to be heading there now."

"Seriously?"

"Yes, that's some coincidence."

"Maybe not. Can you pick me up on your way there? I'll tell you everything when I see you."

I agreed, and I gave Stetson directions on how to get to The Maroon Unicorn. We mostly talked about Lachlan's odd confession and wondered what sort of punishment he'd get.

When we reached the hotel, Jasper was outside waiting for us, and he bounded into the Range Rover with so much exuberance that the vehicle bobbed back and forth so violently that I thought it would flip over a couple of times. Fortunately, the tyres stayed on the ground. Jasper had a small pizza box in one hand and a plastic bottle of Irn-Bru in the other.

"Did you get any rest?" I asked.

"Nope. But I had a couple of energy drinks, and that's just as good."

"No, it isn't," Zabel insisted.

"Relax. You're not my mother. I just need a good breakfast, and I'll be set to go." Pizza is Jasper's preferred way to start the day.

Sanna sniffed. "That odor. What toppings have you put on your pizza today? I hear myself asking, but I know deep in my heart that the answer will not please me."

"This is haggis with roasted potato and a whisky cream sauce. Anybody want a slice?"

"Haggis?" Sanna didn't hold back. "I think you've taken the whole 'when in Scotland' attitude way too far. Just because you can put something on a pizza, that doesn't mean that it's a smart idea."

"Have you ever tried haggis, Mahabir?"

"It's offal stuffed in an animal stomach. I can count myself lucky that our paths have never crossed."

"I like it. It's basically sausage, and sausage has always been an acceptable pizza topping. Back me up here, Addy."

"That's true enough, but sausages have very different flavors, and some don't blend with cheese and tomato sauce as well as others."

"Well, I say it works better than peanut butter and jelly." Jasper took a massive bite that consumed all but the crust of one slice.

After a brief period of quiet, Cian chimed in, saying, "I'd like to try some, please. You caught my attention with the whisky cream sauce." Jasper pushed the box in his direction with a smile, and Cian helped himself with a "Cheers, mate."

"Addy, Zabel? You want some?"

"We've had our breakfast and we don't want to deprive you of yours," Zabel said, speaking for me, not that I minded in this instance.

Jasper is an unsettlingly swift eater, and the slices vanished with shocking rapidity. As he rolled each slice up into cylinders and devoured them, washing them down with gulps of Irn-Bru, he made little grunts and sighs of appreciation.

It didn't take very long for him to scrape the box clean, and once he'd wiped his fingers on a tissue that Zabel thoughtfully provided, I thought the time was ripe to ask him exactly what information he'd thought was so important to share with us.

"Ah, yes. Sorry for the delay, but I needed to get my strength back up after a long night of livestreaming. So, anyway, I was talking to one of my YouTube pop culture discussion colleagues – he lives around here."

"Is that the one who's perpetually intoxicated?" Zabel queried.

"That's the guy. Anyway, I was talking to him about the whole Peerage Maker situation, and he asked me if I had ever heard of the Great Sausage Scandal. I hadn't, so he was gracious enough to educate me. Are any of you familiar with it?"

We all said no, and requested that he enlighten us. After a deep swig of Irn-Bru to clear his throat, he explained, "First, I know that some of you – and by 'some,' I mean Sanna– are going to wonder just where exactly I'm going with this. You'll question the relevance of this narrative to the current case, but I can assure you, it's connected to the Peerage Maker scam, which is connected to Hunniraube Manor, which is connected to the murders. At least I think it is. Bear with me.

"The story of the Great Sausage Scandal is shrouded in mystery and confusion. If you try to do some research on the internet, you're going to find a bunch of contradictory stories connected to the case. Some accounts disagree on the decades when this happened, and others spell names differently. You can get a nasty headache trying to chase down the details, so I'm just going to paint the case in broad brushstrokes here. Trust me, you'll thank me for being vague in places.

"Anyway, this place we're going to now, Boleskine House, by the 1960s, Aleister Crowley, the old diabolist who made the place infamous, was long gone. At that time, the owner of the house was a moderately well-off widow with a bunch of tragedies in her history. The central character in this little drama is Dennis Loraine (no one can agree on how many 'r's and 'n's there were in his name, one or two), an oft-married, oft-divorced con man with a penchant for embellishing his life's story, such as claiming to be descended from aristocracy or being a war hero. He used his dubious charms to wheedle money out of vulnerable people, like setting up fake psychics to get people to hand over their savings, or forming 'partnerships' with businesspeople in financial straits, and then taking over the company. That's how Loraine got control of a modest little butcher shop, which he used as the cornerstone of his new company Royal Victoria Sausages Ltd. He lies to the government, creates a false province for the company, tells them it's been providing meat products to royalty for a century. Before you know it, he's claiming that he's running a huge pig farm on the grounds of Boleskine House, to provide meat for the Royal Victoria Sausages. But how do you plan to make any money when you're not producing any pork, you wonder? The answer is that you sell shares in the non-existent pig farm, and you rope in a celebrity to get people interested. That celebrity was George Sanders, the actor. Any of you familiar with his work?"

I was the only one who nodded "yes." "Sanders is an Oscar-winner for playing the corrupt drama critic Addison DeWitt in the Best Picture-winning movie *All About Eve*. One of his other most famous roles is his voice work as the tiger Shere Khan in the original Disney animated movie *The Jungle Book*. He was known for playing smooth, cultured villains. Incidentally, his brother, who went by the stage name Tom Conway, played Sherlock Holmes alongside Nigel Bruce as Doctor Watson for a season on the radio after Basil Rathbone retired from the role."

"You can link *anything* back to Sherlock Holmes," Zabel murmured with no trace of mockery in her voice, just mild amusement.

"Exactly, Addy," Jasper agreed. "Sanders became the public face of the make-believe pig farm. At least, I *think* it was Sanders. Wikipedia says it was a different entertainer, George Raft, but everybody else I see on the internet says that's wrong. Anyway, the shady company Loraine sets up to oversee the whole scam is called "Cadno," supposedly a reference to George Sanders, who was known for playing the cad in films. He even titled his bibliography *Memoirs of a Professional Cad*. Although another article says there was a different company called "Loch Ness Foods." Anyway, Sanders probably didn't know exactly what was going on, and he was probably just duped into the whole affair because he needed money – he'd made some bad investments and probably lost a bundle in a couple of divorces. Anyway, like most boondoggles of this nature, the truth came out eventually, and everybody involved got a lot of egg on their faces, and there were a *lot* of prominent people who'd gotten caught up in the crazy investment scheme. Sanders was humiliated, struggled financially in the aftermath, and then suffered from serious health problems for the few remaining years of his life. I don't think anybody went to prison, as far as I know, but Loraine's final years were supposedly pretty grim ones. Noel Coward once declared his intention to write a book or a play about the case and call it *The Great Sausage Scandal.*"

Jasper paused, held up a finger, and took a long draught that drained a bottle of Irn-Bru. "So now, you're probably wondering what this means for the current case. Well, a lot of my friends and fellow content creators on YouTube have been snookered into accepting Peerage Maker as one of their sponsors. And so now, a bunch of us have been digging into the background of this company. It's a house of cards. We know that a great big amoral company is behind the general funding and organization of the project and many other shady deals. But the entity that seems to have proposed the idea in the first place is a newly created start-up company, which doesn't seem to have any headquarters or more than a minimal online presence, called Ondac. That's O-N-D-A-C. See what that is?"

"That's "Cadno" spelled backwards," Zabel, Stetson, and I said together.

Stetson grinned. "I like to do the *Jumble* puzzle at breakfast every day back home."

"And that's not all. Who's the supposed CEO of Ondac? A woman who no one's ever heard of. She supposedly has a degree in economics from Cambridge, but I've found no evidence at all of that. The photo of her is a stock picture used for advertising, and the model in it has been tracked down, and she knows nothing about Ondac. The CEO's name is Loraine Dennis. See that? Just like Cadno was reversed, Dennis Loraine was flip-flopped."

"So what does this mean?" Cian asked.

"I can't determine the extent of the link, but whoever is behind it knows a lot about the Great Sausage Scandal. And that person is also a big fan of George Sanders. The board of directors for Ondac? Andrew Lippincott. Benjamin Ballon. Stuyvesant Nicholl. Miles Fairley. Henry Wotton. These are all roles played by Sanders. I don't know what exactly is going on, but this is all connected in some way."

We didn't get very long to reflect on this point, because Stetson had just pulled up in front of a little sign telling us that we had reached Boleskine House. We climbed out of the Range Rover and started looking in all directions.

"Where is he?" Cian wondered.

"No idea. Gavin? Gavin? GAVIN?" Stetson hollered loud enough to be heard across the loch.

"Let's take a look around," Zabel suggested. Without being told to, we split into pairs. Cian and Stetson walked off together, Sanna and Jasper went in the opposite direction, and Zabel and I went towards the charred remains of the house.

"I don't like this one bit," Zabel whispered, even though no one else was around. "This seems very suspicious to me. Why would he invite us here, of all places?"

"Well, technically, Gavin didn't invite us. He invited Stetson and Cian. Which means that he's only expecting them. I don't know if he saw the rest of us and is hiding, now that he's upset that four extra people are here… or if something else is going on here."

"Whatever it is, my feminine intuition is telling me that something weird is in the air. Gavin's a slimy character, and I'd rather climb twenty flights of stairs rather than ride in an elevator alone with him, but I don't know if he's a murderer. I just wish –"

"Hey! Over here! Hurry"

"Down by the water's edge! Quickly!"

We followed the shouts of the Irish brogue and the Texas twang, and in a moment the four of us had joined the writers by the shore of Loch Ness. Both were kneeling by the body of Gavin Ginnungagap, who had the hilt of an elaborately carved knife sticking out of his chest, in the centre of a damp patch of red.

Zabel was the one who called the police, and when they arrived, the wind started to pick up, and though it wasn't actually raining, there was increased dampness in the air, and our coats provided surprisingly little resistance to the chill. We all found ourselves hoping this wouldn't take too long.

We answered the expected questions, and Cian and Stetson were taken off to one side for further interrogation.

The four of us started walking around to stay warm, and after about half an hour, Chief Constable Griogair arrived, and once again, was much politer and understanding that I expected.

"Based on everybody's testimony, the four of you couldn't possibly have killed the victim. He must have died just a few minutes before you arrived here."

"So we're free to go?" Sanna asked.

"Oh, yes. I'm afraid you won't be able to take the Range Rover, and my men will be a bit busy for a while, but I think one of them can drive your to the nearest bust stop and you can make your way to the hotel from there."

Sanna grumbled something unintelligible, but I was more concerned with another issue. "What about Stetson and Cian?"

"I'm afraid they'll be coming to the station for further questions. They were alone for a few moments, and it's certainly possible that they met Mr. Ginnungagap, stabbed him, and pretended to discover the body."

"But why would they do that?" Zabel asked.

"Perhaps it has something to do with a letter that we found in his pocket. I'm afraid I can't show it to you, but I can summarize it for you. The letter was by Mr. Ginnungagap to Mr. Ícidhe and Mr. McLennan. In it, he says he invested a great deal of money in Mr. Ícidhe's latest play and Mr. McLennan's latest movie, and he wasn't pleased with how they were spending it. Unless they both returned all of his money, he was going to initiate legal action."

That made no sense to me. Why would he write one letter to the both of them, instead of one for each man? And why would the letter be in his pocket? If the two of them were prepared to kill him over this, wouldn't he have given them the letter first? And why wouldn't he have told his lawyers to write and send the letter for him?

I didn't ask the chief constable these questions. We were getting along so well, and I didn't want to spoil it by my telling him his job.

"The knife in his chest... was that from the weapons at the manor?" Zabel asked.

"We're looking into that."

He made a few more comments, and then led us to a police car, where an officer was waiting to take us to the bus stop.

"At least we'll be able to get lunch at the hotel," Sanna noted. "Assuming that Abhorson the failed actor turned waiter is still in a good mood."

Just as we all reached the car, raindrops started splattering upon the windows. I hoped that we wouldn't have a long wait at the bus stop. As we climbed into the police car, I turned around and saw Stetson and Cian standing at off to one side, with a constable standing close to them. I could just barely see their faces, but both men looked worried, and I was concerned for them as well.

CHAPTER NINE
Voyage to the Bottom of Loch Ness

We were politely but bluntly dropped off at a bus stop down the road, and provided with a rapidly spoken set of instructions, telling us which bus to take, when to get off, which bus to transfer to, and when to disembark from it. We were also told we'd have to walk about four blocks back to The Maroon Unicorn, though the constable drove off without telling us which direction we'd have to walk.

Sanna belted out a few choice words to a man who was too far away to hear them, while Jasper shivered in his hoodie and walked off to one side, and Zabel made a call on her mobile. It wasn't immediately visible, but the air was filled with tiny droplets of rain that you couldn't see falling from the sky, but you could feel them gradually, imperceptibly soaking your clothing and dampening your skin and hair.

After a couple of minutes, Zabel ended the call. It was clear that she'd been talking to Waldroup, trying to figure out where he and the others had been for the past hour. "Waldroup says that Philly has been resting peacefully since we last saw her."

"That gives her an alibi, but not him, as she can't confirm it," Sanna noted. "Unless he's protecting her."

"Uh-huh. The staff has all been together for a meeting, so they're covered. Presumably, Lachlan's been under the watchful eye of the police. But as for Lord Hunniraube... his nurse thought that he was down for a nap himself, and slipped out to the loo for a moment. Apparently, he pushed a table in front of the door and slipped away. No one's sure what happened to him."

I sighed. "So for all we know, he made his way to Boleskine House, taking a knife from his personal collection with him."

"Exactly. We just don't know." Zabel turned to her left. "Jasper, what are you doing?"

He held out a finger, and from that distance, I thought at first he was making a rude gesture, but then I realized that he was asking her to wait for a minute. He wound up needing three before answering her.

I had thought that he'd been talking to himself, but as he turned and walked towards is, I could see that he was holding his mobile in his hand. "I've been livestreaming," he informed us. "I've been giving my viewers a look at what I've been doing to look into the whole Peerage Maker situation. I'm giving them an update on the murder. It's going over pretty well. There are almost ten thousand people watching right now."

"Right now?" I asked.

"Absolutely. I'm still livestreaming. I want to them to meet you three. I mention you all the time, and now people want to be properly introduced." He held the mobile up to my face. "This is Addy, Sherlock's secretary. You've all been following his career very closely the last several months."

They have? I thought to myself. I was going to have to start watching some of his videos. I wanted to voice these questions, but all I found myself doing was giving a little wave and saying, "Hi. I hope all of you are doing well."

The mobile moved to my left. "And this is Zabel, true crime reporter extraordinaire."

She smiled and nodded. "It's a pleasure."

Jasper took another couple of steps. "And this woman needs no introduction. Sanna –"

"Gimme that." Sanna wrenched the mobile from his hand. "What is the name of all that is holy is wrong with you people? Don't you have anything better to do with your lives than watch a man who thinks breakfast pizza is the most important meal of the day? Can't you –"

"Didn't I tell you about her?" Jasper shouted, trying to snatch back the phone. Sanna held it out of his grasp, while keeping it pointed on her face. "You see what I have to put up with every day?"

Sanna launched into a rant peppered with words that I really don't feel comfortable reprinting here. My grandparents wouldn't approve of my recording that sort of language for posterity. Sanna's lungs used enough air to fill the Goodyear blimp, but eventually she went dry, and she switched off the livestream and threw the mobile at Jasper's chest. The two argued for a bit before the bus arrived, and then they both sulked all of the way back to The Maroon Unicorn.

We realized too late that we got off the bus a bit after our intended stop, and the fact that we had to trudge about half a mile to the hotel did nothing to improve Sanna's and Jasper's moods. The rain was picking up, and by the time we crossed The Maroon Unicorn's threshold, we all needed to change into dry clothes.

About twenty minutes before the end of lunch service, we managed to get ourselves into the dining room. I didn't recognize our waiter at first, until I realized that Abhorson was smiling. I wasn't the only one who seemed rather stunned by the change. I tried to ask how his day had been going without sounding too incredulous that it appeared to be doing well.

"I realized that part of the reason I've been so grouchy lately is that I've given up on my preferred career. So I did a little searching on the internet, and learned that there's a local theatre group that's holding auditions for Noel Coward's *Blithe Spirit* this weekend. I need to dust off my copy of the play to prepare."

"Break a leg," I told him.

"Thank you." He handed out the menus. "Today I recommend the macaroni cheese pie. It's substantial yet also light, and I'd recommend starting with the Scotch broth, which is made with mutton, barley, and assorted vegetables. Just perfect for a cold, rainy day like today. It's served with a side of fatty cutties. Don't let the name put you off. They're currant scones, and not greasy at all. What do you say?"

We looked at each other and then agreed on the recommended meal.

"Doesn't seem like the same guy at all," Sanna commented shortly after Abhorson had returned to the kitchen.

"You seem to have a positive effect on people," Zabel told me.

"Let's hope he stays in a good mood..." I stopped as I saw how hunched over Jasper was. Realizing he was looking at his phone, I asked him, "See something interesting there?"

"I'm looking at the responses to my last livestream. The comments are unbelievable."

"I'm sorry, Jasper," Zabel was sympathetic. "Even after all this time, I know that I get upset when I see a troll criticizing one of my videos."

"That's just it. The responses are overwhelmingly positive. People are really interested in the case. But that's not the real surprise. It's what they're saying about Sanna."

"What about me?" Sanna was understandably defensive.

"It's not unanimous, but about nine out of ten of my viewers... seem to love you. They enjoy your raw, unfiltered take, and they want to see more of you." He looked up at her with what he thought was an ingratiating smile. "Wanna join my livestream tonight?"

"Why would I do that? Do I look like I'm desperate for attention?"

"C'mon, it'll be fun. All you have to do is tell us what you really think about what's on the telly."

"Practically all of it is hot rubbish."

"You'll need to expand on that a bit, but you're heading in the right direction. You'll get a share of all the money viewers donate. And you'll need it while you look for a new job. I really think you've got to give it a try. I can't believe it. All this time, I've been trying to find ways to get more people to tune in, and all this time the answer was right with me in the flat."

Jasper spent the entirety of the meal encouraging Sanna to become a YouTuber, and Sanna kept expressing her horror at the prospect of such a career change. Zabel and I didn't say much. Certainly Zabel couldn't say one word about that particular career path. Personally, I was happy to have a little break from the case and I found their interplay to be a welcome distraction from murdered Monster Hunterz in the car with us.

Just as we were finishing up our meal, we heard screams coming from the kitchen. The four of us left the last few bites on our plates and followed the noise. The chef, a woman with grey hair and a white jacket, was standing by the door, clearly in a state of shock. Zabel gently took her shoulders and led her to a chair, and while she tried to calm her down, the rest of us went out the door.

Abhorson was lying on the ground, beside the rubbish bins. There was a large wound running from the left side of his forehead to the temple, and a bloodstained whisky bottle with a long crack on it lay on the ground a few feet away from him. A bag of garbage lay next to his right hand. There were a series of fractures across the glass, and I couldn't tell if they were caused by the bottle striking Abhorson's head, or when the bottle had been dropped. There was neither sight nor sound of the assailant.

"Another murder," Jasper muttered.

I knelt down and felt his pulse. "It's not a murder yet. He's still breathing." I quickly called 999.

Zabel stepped out the door. "The chef says she asked Abhorson to take out the kitchen waste. Then she heard something odd and went outside. She saw someone in a balaclava standing over him, and was about to strike again, when she started screaming. I guess that scared off the assailant."

"This is connected to the other murders, right?" Jasper asked.

"I'm still not ready to rule out the possibility of a disgruntled former restaurant customer," Sanna retorted.

I said nothing, as I was trying to coax a recent memory out from the recesses of my mind. I was still thinking when the paramedics and the police arrived. I'd stayed with Abhorson, who had started making unintelligible groans and sighs. He wasn't coherent, but his pulse was still strong. Zabel stayed with the chef, and Sanna took a quick walk around the inn, checking to see if there were any sign of the assailant. She'd armed herself with a marble rolling pin from the kitchen. Jasper had returned to the dining room, having mumbled something about there being no point in allowing the rest of our food to go to waste. It was only later, after the police had questioned me that I realized that he'd been doing more livestreaming, talking about the case for the benefit of his subscribers.

After being out in the rain, I was once again soaked through and feeling a chill coming on. I returned to my room, showered with the hottest temperature water that I could endure, and donned a fresh jumper and trousers. I hoped that I wouldn't be caught out in another downpour. I only had a few more changes of clean clothes left. Either the case would need to be resolved soon, or I'd need to find a laundromat in Inverness. As I drew the cold out of my bones, I reflected on the events of the last two days, and I started coming up with a theory that seemed pretty outlandish, even to my over-imaginative mind. Still, it wouldn't be too difficult to confirm or refute some of my ideas.

Returning downstairs, my friends were back at the table. The chef appreciated our looking out for Abhorson, Zabel explained, and she'd provided us with a complementary plate of Millionaire's Shortbread. This was a triple-layer treat, consisting of a square of shortbread, covered with caramel, and topped off with a thick covering of chocolate. As I ate two pieces, Zabel explained that she'd called Waldroup again. Philly was still sleeping and Lord Hunniraube was still on the lam.

"Do you think Lord Hunniraube did this?" I hesitated to answer Jasper's question, not because I wasn't sure of my answer, but because I wasn't certain if he was still livestreaming or not. After Sanna assured me that she had given Jasper a choice between turning off his mobile or having that mobile placed in a rather delicate portion of his anatomy, I felt comfortable enough to say that I had a pretty shaky theory of what had happened. I took out my mobile and did a little searching.

"See this theatre's website?" I passed my device around. "Take a look at these cast photos."

Zabel squinted. "Is that… Holy cow, it is."

"Let me see." Sanna took my mobile next, followed by Jasper. "Wow. What made you think to look this up?"

"Something Abhorson said this morning, along with a couple of bits of information connected to the Peerage Maker scam." I started tapping as quickly as I could. "I need to send this picture to our old pal Inspector Dankworth. If he gives me the answer I think he will, then I think we have our killer. There's a lot of additional information to be proven, but the police can handle that."

"But even if you're right, what's the motive?"

I brainstormed aloud for a bit, before expounding upon my farfetched theory yet.

"I like that," Zabel said. "It seems a bit improbable, but this whole case has been crazy pants."

"How do you think you're going to prove it?" Sanna asked.

"I think as soon as the rain lets up, we need to rent a boat and go out on Loch Ness," I explained. After doing a little more internet searching, I found the map I wanted. "This is where the prop Nessie from *The Private Life of Sherlock Holmes* rests at the bottom of the loch. Now we just have to hire a diver. Unless one of you has experience with scuba diving. I certainly don't."

"I don't either," Sanna said.

"Don't look at me," Jasper shook his head.

"I've scuba dived a few times," Zabel replied. "Once when my family took a holiday to Jamaica and a couple of times when I've visited the Mediterranean."

"Are you up for it again now?" I asked.

"Definitely!"

My mobile chimed, and I told the others that the text was from Inspector Dankworth.

"Well? What does it say?" Sanna has many lovely qualities, but patience isn't one of them.

"He says that he's never seen the person in question in his life." I was about to call him, but then I realized that there was a chance that someone might overhear. I rushed upstairs and talked to Inspector Dankworth in the privacy of my room.

"What did he say? Zabel asked.

"He says he's on his way and told us not to do anything stupid or reckless."

"Hmm."

"I don't like that 'Hmm,' Carvalho."

"No reason why you should. But now I'm looking forward to a little scuba diving. I'm going to look into where I might be able to rent some equipment."

"But if we just wait for the authorities…" I started.

"I just want to take a look. If we put this theory forward and it turns out we're wrong, we'll look like a pack of fools."

"It's my theory," I reminded Zabel. "If I've gone horribly far afield, then that's on me."

"I'm dating you, and this reflects on me as well. If *we're*, yes, *we're* wrong, I lose my credibility as a journalist. I just want to take a look, just so we don't become laughingstocks."

Before I said anything else, I took a good, long look at Zabel's face, and I could see the resoluteness. I debated saying something else, and decided against it. Besides, I wanted to see if there was anything to my theory as well.

Jasper looked up from his mobile. "The weather report says that the rain's going to let up in about half an hour before starting up again around sundown and proceeding intermittently through the night. If we're going to do this, it ought to be now."

And so, we took a bus down the coast of the lake, and quickly maxed out my credit card renting a boat, an underwater camera, and a diving suit for Zabel. As I signed the receipt, I heard a little thought in my head, saying, *"This is dumb. Really dumb. What are you going to do if you're wrong? You're putting two and two together and getting five. No, five million. Back out of this, see if you can get your money back, and keep your dignity."*

This little mental battle raged inside my skull for an indeterminate amount of time, and just as I made up my mind to back out of the whole deal, I realized that I was no longer on dry land. I was riding along in a boat, with a life vest around my neck, and I wasn't really certain how I'd gotten there. Zabel was standing next to me, wearing a dark red and blue scuba suit, and she looked so great in it I almost suggested that she add it to her regular wardrobe rotation before I remembered that it wasn't the sort of outfit one could really wear as part of your ordinary routine.

Sanna stood with her arms crossed. "I think we're making fools of ourselves," she said, reading my mind.

"Cheer up! No matter what happens, we're having a smashing day out on Loch Ness. Look at that view! Fell the wind on your face! Enjoy it!" Jasper said, steering the boat towards our destination.

"Who are you to lecture me about taking pleasure in being outdoors! How the hell many times have you left your room in the last two years?" Sanna challenged him.

"Fair enough. I admit that I've been a bit housebound lately. Maybe I'll have to rethink a few aspects of my schedule when we get home."

I wasn't aware that Jasper even had a driving license. "Have you ever steered a boat before?"

"Oh, yes. I used to go fishing with my grandfather all the time, and he taught me how to drive his boat." Another bit of Jasper's backstory that I'd never known about until that moment.

"How far are we from the site?" Zabel asked.

"I'd say we're about five minutes away."

Zabel nodded. "Addy, Sanna, please help me hook up this tank." She pinned up her hair and covered it, and after an embarrassing attempt where we tried to put the tank on upside-down, we finally managed to put everything where it needed to be.

"Don't forget those little tracking devices we bought," Sanna reminded her, handing her a little bag.

"Thanks. I don't want to find what we're looking for and then be unable to locate it again."

"Hmm..." I said, looking across the loch.

"What's the problem?" Zabel inquired.

"I think that boat over there is following us."

"Probably not," Jasper assured us. "It's most likely a tour boat trawling for Nessie."

The little knot in my belly remained unappeased, and I couldn't help but wonder if something were wrong. I knew my mind was distracted by the fact that I hadn't noticed the headband Jasper was wearing until now. There was a little camera strapped to his forehead. "Are you livestreaming this?" I asked.

"No, just recording the video. The wind's so strong it's going to mess up any attempt to record the sound, so I'll dub over it later."

"Assuming of course that we find something worth publicizing," I noted.

"Oh, we're going to find something. I'm sure of it." Jasper's confidence was very strong, and I wished that I could have shared it. A few moments later he stopped the boat. "All right, according to the GPS system, we are here. The remains of Billy Wilder's failed Loch Ness Monster prop should lie almost directly beneath us. And maybe something else. We'll find out."

"This is a bad idea. This is a bad idea. This is a bad idea..." I found myself muttering.

"Relax. If all I get out of this are a few photographs of the sunken fake Nessie, we're still way ahead of the game. They're the perfect souvenir, and they'll make for the basis of a brilliant video." Zabel gave me a quick peck on the cheek. "All right. Say a prayer, wish me luck, and let's get going!"

Before I knew it, Zabel had pulled her goggles over her eyes, adjusted her breathing apparatus, and was in the waters of Loch Ness. I suddenly panicked, worrying that something could go wrong with the scuba equipment, endangering my girlfriend. As I tried to steady and deepen my breathing, I felt Sanna's hand on my shoulder, giving me a violent shake.

"Addy? I think you're right about that boat. It's coming straight towards us, and it's not slowing down at all."

Jasper, who'd been sipping a bottle of Irn-Bru, jumped into action. "Evasive maneuvers!" He restarted the engine, and steered the boat off to the side.

The other boat similarly adjusted its course. The second boat was a bit smaller than ours, but it was faster and nimbler. Now that it was just fifty yards away from us, I could see the person driving the boat was wearing a black balaclava. "He's got a spear gun!" I shouted.

"Serpentine! Serpentine!" Jasper roared, as he started weaving our boat back and forth, leaving a massive bubbly wake behind us. The spear gun fired as Sanna and

I both fell to the deck, and I screamed at Jasper to do the same. As it turned out, it wasn't necessary. The spear missed Jasper by a couple of yards, eventually falling to the surface of the loch a short distance away.

By now, the other boat was only about twenty feet away from us, and our boat was far slower and moved more awkwardly in the water. "I think he's going to try to ram us!"

"I can see that, Addy," a testy Sanna responded. "I have a plan. Stand up and get ready to jump. We've got one shot to take him down."

"What?"

"If you miss, kick off your shoes and try to swim for shore. Are you ready?" Despite Jasper's best steering, the attacking boat was now ten feet from us and headed right where we were standing.

"Get ready, Addy," Sanna snarled. "I'll aim for him. You grab the steering wheel. Got it? Go!" Sanna vaulted over the edge and flung herself with more momentum than I thought was physically possible for her. Before I could warn her that the masked man had a knife, she was soaring through the air, and I found myself jumping, only to realize to my horror that my foot had caught against the side of the boat and I wasn't going to travel as far as I'd hoped. I wasn't able to land inside the attacking vessel, but I landed with a bruising blow upon the bow, and I gripped the slick surface as best I could in an attempt to keep from rolling off into the water.

"Sanna! Are you all right?"

"Get over here and help me!"

I inched my way forward along the bow, until I could see Sanna on top of the masked figure, her left hand gripping his right wrist, struggling to get him to drop the knife.

We hit a massive wave, and I nearly rolled right off the boat, but I was able to grab a little bit of projecting metal, and using all my strength, I launched myself over the windshield, bruising myself further along the way. There was a large tackle box on the ground next to me, and without thinking, I grabbed it and hurled it at the knife. The blow knocked the weapon from the attacker's grip, and it skittered across the deck.

Somehow, I managed to fight through the pain and get to my feet. I staggered over and grabbed the arms of the masked man.

"Thanks, Addy," Sanna grunted, just as she delivered a roundhouse punch to our opponent's masked face. He groaned and lay still, and Sanna adjusted herself so she was seated on his chest, with her hands pinning his arms. "Now grab the wheel before we crash."

We were headed straight for our boat, but I zigged and Jasper zagged, and we avoided a collision by mere inches. A moment later we both stopped our boats, and we bobbed gently in the loch as I waited for my pulse to slow to a much more reasonable three hundred beats a minute.

I looked around for a bit of rope or something similar in order to save Sanna from having to keep pinning our would-be killer from getting free, but there was nothing. "Will you be able to stay like that until we get to shore?" I asked her.

"If he wakes up I can always punch him again."

Now that we were out of danger, I started worrying about Zabel. We were probably at least two hundred yards from where we left her, and I realized that she almost certainly had no idea that we had just been attacked..

Time passed. I asked Sanna if she wanted to switch places, but she declined, informing me that she wanted full credit for taking down the killer. "Shall I take off his balaclava?" she asked. I wondered why we hadn't done that earlier, but before we ripped off his mask, we heard a splash from about two hundred and fifty yards away. Zabel turned around, saw us and started swimming towards us. Jasper eased the boat towards her and helped her back aboard.

Once Jasper brought the boat back within easy hearing distance, a jubilant Zabel shouted, "I found both of them, Addy! You were right!"

A minute earlier, I'd genuinely believed that my theory had been a horribly misguided fever dream. "Are you serious?"

"Yes! I found the Nessie prop from *The Private Life of Sherlock Holmes*. I took pictures, too, and put a tracking device on it. Then I started moving outwards in a spiral, searching the floor of the loch, and I finally discovered a large lump of plastic wrap. I wiped off some algae, and there was a dead body in it! It's just as you thought! Although the body was so decomposed, I have no idea who it was in there. But I put a tracker on it as well."

"Well, I suppose it's possible that someone else murdered somebody I've never heard of and threw the body in the loch, but as long as I'm on a lucky streak, I'm going to keep backing my far-out theory and put my money on the theory that the corpse belongs to the *real* Chief Constable Griogair."

Sanna ripped off the balaclava and tossed it off to one side. I didn't mind, as I figured that she deserved those honours. I gazed down and felt the sweet rush of vindication that comes from making a correct series of deductions about a crime. The unconscious face of the man until quite recently I had thought of as Chief Constable Griogair confirmed all of my suspicions.

CHAPTER TEN

All the Answers

The next several hours were not particularly easy or pleasant. The Inverness police did not immediately embrace the idea that their chief constable was an imposter and a murderer, and when he regained consciousness, Griogair told them that we had attacked him for no good reason. When we asked why he had taken a boat out to the middle of Loch Ness while wearing a balaclava, he was at a loss to respond, but his silence didn't allay the hostility of the representatives of the forces of law and order. Only Jasper showing them the footage of a masked man wearing the same clothes that Griogair was currently sporting trying to ram his boat into ours turned the tide in our favour.

We were separated and questioned for quite some time. At first my theories were met with skepticism, even derision. Zabel must have gotten the police to look at her photographs of the sunken corpse, because after twenty minutes, someone burst into the interrogation room, whispered something into my questioners' ears, and it led to a dramatic change in their attitude.

I explained my theory, peppering it with qualifiers and explaining the logic behind my deductions at length. Eventually, I was left alone for an uncomfortably long time, then questioned some more, and by ten that night, the four of us were thanked for our trouble and politely asked to stay in Inverness, as we would almost certainly need to answer more questions tomorrow.

"Not before noon. I'm wiped and I need my sleep." Sanna spoke with such finality that the policeman who was speaking to us found himself unable to respond verbally. Once again, we relied on the bus to take us back to The

Maroon Unicorn. Zabel, who at some point must have been given the opportunity to change out of her scuba suit, fell asleep on my shoulder for a brief nap. As my eye fell upon the bag that I'd helped her carry onto the bus, I looked inside and saw the scuba suit in it. I remembered that Zabel had left the air tanks on the boat, and that as far as I knew, the rental boat remained moored to a pier. With a sudden lurch in my belly, I remembered that we were supposed to have the boat and equipment back by sundown. Would there be penalties? Could we get a note from the police, telling the rental shop to waive any fines due to extenuating circumstances? For the sake of my bank account, I certainly hoped so. And what about the rented underwater camera? Could they be holding it as evidence?

Sanna was in the seat in front of me, and after I whispered my concerns to her, she replied with a dismissive, "Relax, Zhuang. I've taken care of it. The police called the shop and we won't have to deal with any late fees. They've sent someone to pick up the boat, also."

That was a load off my mind. Soon afterwards, we reached our stop, and I awakened Zabel.

"How late is the hotel restaurant open?" Jasper asked.

With the realization that my belly was uncomfortably empty, I remembered that the last seating was at nine. As we looked along the street, most of the shops seemed to be closed. Jasper's nose, thankfully, is well trained for tracking down quick service, and he managed to find a little place one block over from our route to the hotel. As they only took cash, and I was the only one with a full wallet, I paid for the overflowing bags of assorted curries, doner kebabs, and bottled beverages which of course included Jasper's new life's blood, Irn-Bru.

We were hoping we could slip into the little private dining room unnoticed, but when we pulled open the hotel's front door, we saw Waldroup, Philly, Cian, Stetson, the front desk clerk, the cook, and Abhorson, who was sitting in a corner with a bandaged head, though he was otherwise looking well.

The moment we entered the room, we were hit by a volley of questions from everybody else. It was impossible to respond with all of the voices speaking at once. Finally, when the others had quieted down and there was a brief moment of silence, Jasper had a question of his own.

"Can we eat first before we say anything?" The man knew his priorities. Frankly, given the growling in my stomach, I was with him one hundred percent. The killer was in the hands of the authorities, and we had to leave the one outstanding issue, finding the missing Lord Hunniraube, to the police, though we could attend to our own hunger.

At first, the cook was a bit miffed at the thought at another restaurant's food being eaten in her dining room, but when she realized that the alternative was reopening her kitchen and preparing a meal for the four of us, her asperity melted away, and she even provided us with plates and silverware.

Solving crimes and nearly escaping an attempt on our lives gave all of us powerful appetites, and we tucked into our take-aways with relish. The food was nothing special, but there's something oddly satisfying about cheap food that's heavily seasoned and glistening with oil, especially when you're very hungry. I would have enjoyed it more if not for all of the pairs of eyes fixed on, waiting for us to finish.

The food sat heavily on our stomachs, and it wasn't long before three of us were sated. The attentive reader will deduce at once that the member of our group who kept on eating was Jasper, who was currently on his third helping of everything and still going strong. As we didn't have a little refrigerator in our room, there was actually some justification for his continued consumption. Anything he didn't eat would spoil.

"Are you done with your munchy boxes?' an obviously impatient Waldroup asked.

"Munchy boxes?" Zabel asked, clearly not familiar with the term.

"What you're eating there. Kind of like a pizza box, only filled with kebab meat and curry and chips and perhaps a few other items, depending on the establishment selling the food. Sometimes there's a bit of salad so there's something healthy, though it's usually not that good for you because by the time you get it home, the lettuce is drenched in sauce and grease."

"I see." I had noticed a bit of greenery in a corner of my box, but as it was really closer to wilted brownery, I had dismissed it as a sad attempt at garnish and left it untouched.

"Well, now that we've answered one of your questions, would you mind answering some of ours?" Philly asked, with palpable annoyance in her tone.

"What did you want to know?" I asked.

"Everything! What happened today?"

Zabel and Sanna nodded in my direction, indicating that they expected me to tell the story, especially as Sanna seemed to have gotten a second wind and had helped herself to more food, and was now engaging in a stare-down with Jasper over the last samosa. So I did. I started recounting everything that had happened since that morning. It took the better part of an hour, but I managed to keep everybody's attention, even Cian and Stetson, who had actually been there for many of the events that I was describing.

"But I don't understand," Waldrop frowned. "Whose body was at the bottom of the loch?"

"It was the real Chief Constable Griogair. The killer murdered him some months ago and assumed his identity."

"But who is this guy?" Philly asked.

"I don't know his name, just that he's the long-lost father of your uncle Lachlan. I saw a picture of him, but he wasn't named. Right now, I only have some rough deductions as to what happened, but if you're willing to listen to my theories, and if you'll be forgiving should any of my conclusions be proven wrong at some point in the future, I'll be happy to tell you what I think led up to the crimes."

Everybody nodded, and I launched into my explanation of the case. As it turned out, I was about ninety-five percent correct. For the sake of clarity and personal ego, I have corrected all the parts of my theory that proved to be a bit off the mark. I've also filled in some background details that I didn't know at the time.

"Well, for the benefit of those of you who don't know the background of the Hunniraube family lineage, I'll tell you that the late Lady Hunniraube – Philly's grandmother, I mean – was married twice. Her first wedding was an elopement to a poor actor. By 'poor,' I mean, 'having little money.' Nothing to do with his talent.

He must have been pretty skilled, actually, in order to pull off the deception for so long. Anyway, he married Lady Hunniraube, or rather, whatever her maiden name was. She had a son with him, Lachlan, but after being raised in comfort all of her life, she decided that living close to the bone in the theatre world wasn't for her. I'm sure her family put pressure on her, and if she sensed the darkness and instability in him, well I don't think she needed too much encouragement to file for an annulment – I'm not sure how her family managed it, but perhaps she was underage when they married. That or some other legal technicality."

Zabel joined the summation. "I bet that Lady Hunniraube's family either paid him off handsomely or threatened him to go away, and for whatever reason, he conceded. He signed away all rights to keep his son, and he moved away to pursue his stage career. Well, he wasn't nearly as successful as he'd dreamed. He'd managed to keep getting parts in small productions here and there, but he never became the big star he dreamed of being. I think that his disappointments and thwarted ambitions weighed pretty heavily on him, and I think that it warped his psyche a lot. He probably felt like he'd been cheated out of his marriage and his son, and his middling acting career just poured gasoline on the flames. Over the years, the resentments just got worse and worse, and at some point a year or more ago, he decided that he was going to get his revenge.

It was too late to take out his fury on his ex-wife or her second husband. They'd been dead for a long time. But the current Lord Hunniraube's… eccentricities were becoming well-known. And I think that our murderer turned his bitterness and hatred towards the man who, in his view, was the son of the man who had stolen his wife and child. Lord Hunniraube had been raised like a princeling, and Lachlan's status had always been second-class in that family. So after decades of antipathy, an angry man decided to get his revenge. He believed that everything had been taken from him, so now he was going to take everything from the current Lord Hunniraube – his money, his reputation, his manor… even his freedom."

"Why not just kill him?" Abhorson wondered.

"I think he thought that was too merciful," I answered. "Lord Hunniraube is an obsessed man, but the pseudo-Griogair was equally single-minded in his quest for vengeance. He wanted Lord Hunniraube humiliated and impoverished. Losing his wife and son was an ego blow that never healed. Fake Griogair had lived with his anger for more than forty years, and he had an appetite for destruction. I wonder if he had a plan to enrich his son, as well. I doubt it, given the fact that he never tried to reunite with Lachlan. I guess he didn't want to actually reforge a relationship with his son, so perhaps he put revenge over family. From what I can tell, Lachlan had no idea that his father was even alive, let alone in town, killing people, and coming after the Hunniraube estate." I was going quite a bit beyond the reasonable conclusions of logic and moving into pop psychology, but the further investigations of the police wound up justifying my conclusions, luckily for my reputation as a sleuth.

Waldroup was looking confused. "Wait a minute. I'm not clear on how exactly he took over the real Chief Constable Griogair's life."

"Quite frankly, neither am I. I know that their paths must have crossed somehow. I think that the imposter must have been looking for a way to integrate himself into Inverness and start the process of destroying Lord Hunniraube. My guess is that as he was developing his plans, he initially intended to create some fictitious alter ego and to stay under the radar. Then he met the real Griogair, and decided that it would be better to take over an existing person's identity, especially someone in a position of authority. I don't know how they met, but I have one wild guess that could be totally wrong, though it's the only idea I have that's based on any tangible evidence.

"When I first met the man calling himself Griogair, I noticed a Gamblers Anonymous chip on his keychain. What if the imposter met the real Griogair at GA? Maybe by a twist of fate, one was even the other's sponsor? That would explain how he might have known so many details about the real Griogair's life. People can share a lot when they're helping each other recover from addiction. Maybe it was a total accident, maybe the impostor manipulated himself into the policeman's life somehow. I don't know, but I think that when a man with no close family was being transferred to Inverness, where no one knew him or had met him in-person, the impostor jumped at the chance to take over his identity."

"That was quite a risk," Sanna objected. "I know that it's not uncommon for senior police officers to be transferred to strange cities, but surely someone would have caught him sooner rather than later."

"I agree, it couldn't have lasted forever, but it's only been a few months. And remember, we're still living in a world that's recovering from the effects of the pandemic. Think about it. People aren't travelling around as much. If he wanted to wear a mask in public in order to disguise his features, people wouldn't tell him to remove it. His makeup skills were strong and his vocal mimicry was excellent. More often than not, all conversations with members of the police force who actually knew Griogair wouldn't be in person, but through video chat. He could always say that they were having technical difficulties with their Internet – as indeed, he did to us. An adjustment to the camera to make it extra fuzzy, or perhaps he just disabled it and told people it wasn't working… it wouldn't be too challenging to hide his face for extended periods of time. He probably did a convincing job mimicking Griogair's voice."

I took a deep sip of water before continuing. "Before I continue, I have to admit that I'm not sure what the fake Griogair's real name is, but I believe that Abhorson knows."

"What!" A bit of the old asperity crept back into Abhorson's demeanor. "Are you insinuating that I had something to do with this?"

"Oh, no, no, no. Nothing like that. I'm simply stating that you worked with him. I mean you acted with him in a musical. That's why he attacked you, incidentally. He knew that you were here in town, and he was pretty close to achieving his goals. However, he was also increasingly paranoid that something might go wrong, so he overreacted and went after you. That was Sanna's fault, incidentally. Not that she meant to cause you harm, but she mentioned your name in front of him when we were at Boleskine House, and since there aren't many Abhorsons, he wondered if he might bump into an old co-star at a most inconvenient time. He did a little reconnaissance, recognized you, and decided that Inverness wasn't big enough for the both of you. He gave you a nasty conk on the head, and he probably would have kept bludgeoning you until he killed you if the chef hadn't shown up and caused a distraction that wound up saving your life."

"Thanks," Abhorson told the chef.

"Not at all," she replied.

"But wait a minute," Abhorson told me, "what show did I do with him?"

"If I'm right – and I admit it's a stretch – it was *Applause*. You told me you were in that."

"Why do you think it was that show?" Philly asked. "I've never heard of it."

"Because *Applause* is the musical version of the classic movie *All About Eve*."

"I'm not familiar with that film, either."

"Well, I don't need to go into the plot. All you need to know is that the actor George Sanders was in it, and he was involved in the Great Sausage Scandal at Boleskine House. *Applause* has some major character changes from *All About Eve* due to copyright reasons – they had to base their show on the original short story that inspired the movie, and they couldn't use the characters that were in the film and not the short story. So the movie's character of the suspicious assistant Birdie Coonan was replaced with the gay hairdresser Duane Fox –"

"My role," Abhorson nodded.

"Right. And the corrupt critic Addison de Witt was turned into the theatrical producer Howard Benedict."

Abhorson thought for a moment and then pulled the name out of his memory. "The actor who played that part was Iagan MacCaa,"

Zabel's fingers fluttered across the screen of her mobile, and she worked her magic on the search engine, bringing up the uncaptioned publicity photographic from the production of *Applause* in question. She showed it to Abhorson. "That's him."

"That's the man we knew as Griogair." Zabel showed his picture to the others. "He shaved his beard, dyed his hair, and altered his features with a little makeup, but that's him."

"Makeup, of course." Another piece clicked into place for me. "When I first met him, I noticed all of these little red dots on his face. I thought he'd blown some blood vessels in a fit of temper, but now I think that it was a reaction to wearing makeup all the time for his disguise. Wearing it all day, even if it was subtle enough not to be noticed by the real policemen, probably caused some breakouts on his cheeks.

"Anyway, it just made sense to me that Griogair– I mean, MacCaa– would have played a role based on the character made famous by George Sanders. I figured that MacCaa did a bunch of research on Sanders before the show as he was getting into character, and that's how he learned about the Great Sausage Scandal." A few of the others expressed curiosity on this point, and I quickly summarized the story. "At the time, he probably didn't think that he'd ever use a comparable scam in his personal revenge scheme, but he filed the story away for future reference."

"So when did he kill the real Griogair?" the desk clerk asked.

"It must have happened before the genuine Griogair had the chance to meet anybody. I expect he needed to keep him alive for some reason, and then at some point up here he murdered Griogair – I don't know how." (The autopsy later proved that the real Griogair had died from a blow to the head.) "Then he assumed his identity, wrapped up the body, and dropped it into Loch Ness, where he believed that no one would ever find it. Meanwhile, he started his plan to use the Peerage Maker business to create a scandal that would humiliate and destroy Lord Hunniraube." I rapidly explained how the Peerage Maker scam worked, and how he must have paired up with the shady company that specialized in undertakings like this, taking submitted ideas, funding them, and then paying the person who submitted the suggestion a share of the profits. MacCaa had created the fake company Ondac as a shield, but the Easter eggs connected to the Great Sausage Scandal wound up pointing right in his direction.

"But a few months later," I continued, "he realized that through a one-in-ten thousand chance, he'd left the body in a place where it stood a very real risk of being discovered."

"That's when the Monster Hunterz came to town," Zabel chimed in. "They talked about finding the Loch Ness Monster prop from *The Private Life of Sherlock Holmes*, and at some point in one of their public presentations, MacCaa must have seen their maps, and realized to his horror that by through some twist of fate, he'd dropped the body a stone's throw from the location of the sunken prop. About a hundred yards away, by my estimate. It was easy enough to overlook if you weren't looking for it, but MacCaa didn't know that. He just knew that if the Monster Hunterz got too close, they'd find the remains of the real Griogair, and that meant exposure for him."

"Exactly," I nodded. "So he killed them. Again, I don't know how." (The autopsies later proved that the Monster Hunterz had also been bludgeoned to death.) "This time, it didn't matter if the bodies were found, and I think he decided that it would actually be a *good* thing if the corpses were discovered. When he'd started his plans, he didn't know the state of Lord Hunniraube's mind – Philly does her best to keep it quiet, and I'd wager that a lot of the people in town have too much sensitivity to gossip – and he later learned a lot of people would have questioned the theory that Lord H. was capable of trying to make a quick pound off of unethical practices. But the idea that he'd snapped, turned violent, and attacked two men because he thought they were going to find the Loch Ness Monster before he did? That was more believable. So he broke into the shed – he'd found out about the freezers at some point during reconnaissance on the estate, and hid the bodies there, expecting that they'd be discovered soon and that all fingers would point towards Lord Hunniraube. By a fluke, they were bent up enough for their frozen bodies for both of them to fit snugly in a car boot.

But imagine how shocked he must have been when his own flesh and blood threw a spanner into his plans! MacCaa assumed that anybody who discovered the bodies would call the police immediately and assume that Lord Hunniraube did it. He never dreamt that his long-estranged son, Lachlan, would decide to hush up a scandal, and hide the bodies in Zabel's car. And then to tell the police, all so the corpses would be discovered far away from Hunniraube Manor! I'll bet MacCaa was flabbergasted and furious. Here he is trying to ruin Hunniraube Manor's reputation, and Lachlan's inadvertently undone his efforts.

Of course, MacCaa didn't know that his son had moved the bodies. I think he was totally confused, and he lacked the professional investigative training that could've helped him solve the case on his own. Now he was in a pickle. He had hoped that the remains of the Monster Hunterz would be found in the deep freezes, and that it would be easy to pin the blame directly on the laird of the manor. Now there was an added complication, and he was stuck in the position of hoping that the police officers under his supervision would find out who had moved the bodies, and still conclude that Lord Hunniraube was responsible for their deaths. For all he knew, Lord Hunniraube had planted the bodies and sent the note himself."

"He should have realized that it couldn't have been Lord H. due to his injured arm," Zabel reminded me.

"You're right. Of course, we don't know if MacCaa was sharp enough to realize that. He was never a brilliant criminal mastermind – all his plans were based more on luck and opportunity than careful preparation. I think that he just came up with a scheme and expected that everything would work out directly to his advantage. And then everything started falling apart, and he began spiraling out of control. I didn't realize it at the time, but when we discovered the bodies, he made a big mistake."

"What was that?" Waldroup asked.

"He was way too nice to us. Much too understanding. I know that Zabel and I are clearly not the homicidal type, but you'd think he'd be sure to hold us for questioning, and at the very least, he ought to be a lot more suspicious of us. I'm not sure, but I don't think that he was following proper police protocol with us. I think it was a combination of him knowing for certain that we had nothing to do with the deaths, plus the fact that he wanted all of the suspicion directly on Lord Hunniraube, that led to him behaving as his did. After all, if he'd arrested us or even detained us, we would have been an unwelcome distraction. There was only one man who MacCaa wanted as a suspect. So he let us go on our own recognizance and was surprisingly patient waiting for our attorney to let us speak, because he just wasn't interested in what we had to say. For all he knew, we could say something that might inadvertently point the finger of suspicion towards him, or at least, away from his preferred suspect."

Abhorson nodded. "When I worked with MacCaa, I noticed that he was pretty solid when he had a script to follow, but he could not, for the life of him, improvise. When we were acting together, the actress playing Margo Channing kept fumbling her lines, saying something a little different from how it was written, or coming up with something extemporaneous and funny. And then when the audience stopped laughing, he'd be lost, and the other actors would have to say his line for him or whisper a prompt in his ear or something else, just to keep the show moving. He wasn't a bad actor at all – he was quite skilled at inhabiting his character, really. But I would think that he'd have been happier pursuing a career in film or television, where everything is recorded in little takes in a controlled environment. He just wasn't made for the unpredictability of live theatre."

"He wasn't half bad at interactive drama at first," Zabel opined, "but the narrative spiraled out of his control, and he didn't have a sufficiently firm grasp of his character and how he should act in certain situations. I dare say he should've done more research, but I suspect was too impatient to get to his plan."

"What happened to all of the money he made from the whole Peerage Maker plan?" Philly wondered.

We didn't have an answer for that question then, but we found out a bit later that the shady corporation that had funded the project had lived up to its reputation for dirty dealings, and had only given him a tiny fraction of the lucre they amassed over the last several months. He'd kept a bit of it for personal expenses, but he'd digitally transferred the vast majority of it from an account with Ondac's name on it into a bank account in Philly's name, all in an attempt to frame her for involvement in the scam and further humiliate the name of Hunniraube.

The company funding Peerage Maker, was, once again, a legally amorphous entity of dubious location. The authorities were unable to charge anybody connected with the corporation with any crime, though a few days after the details of MacCaa's misdeeds hit the news, the Peerage Maker website vanished. Despite the publicity connected to the case, and numerous YouTube videos educating people about the realities of the situation, there are still thousands of people around the world insisting that they have a legal right to be referred to as Lord or Lady Such-and-Such. It has led to a number of frustrating and at times hilarious incidents, including a group of individuals from Sioux Falls, South Dakota, who were under the impression that thanks to making a purchase from Peerage Maker, they now had the right to sit in the House of Lords and vote on laws affecting the United Kingdom. One of them even sought the advice of a solicitor to have himself installed in that branch of Parliament, and when he was gently informed that he had purchased a worthless piece of paper that provided him with no rights or privileges of the nobility, he became enraged. He promptly stormed out of that solicitor's office, and then went on to seek legal guidance from no fewer than eight other solicitors, all of whom provided him with similar opinions. None of them ever received a penny for their time and trouble, and none of them wanted to deal with the hassle of trying to use the majesty of the law to force him to pay his bill for the consultation. Indeed, one of the solicitors happily paid for the ticket to send the frustrated fellow back to Sioux Falls.

"So I understand why MacCaa killed the real Griogair and the Monster Hunterz," said Cian, "but what about Gavin? What did he do?"

I shrugged. "My theory is that Gavin was out for a stroll in the woods a week earlier, and he saw MacCaa carrying the bodies to the shed. They were probably wrapped up in a tarp or something like that, so he didn't realize what it was at the time. But later, after news of the Monster Hunterz was released, Gavin put two and two together, and I bet he blackmailed him."

"He can't have expected to extort much money from a copper," Cian argued. "And Gavin made a bundle from his books."

"Who said anything about wanting money?" Sanna asked. "From what I've heard about Gavin's reputation, his preferred deadly sin was lust, not greed. Perhaps he told Griogair– I mean, MacCaa– just what he wanted in exchange for keeping his silence, and MacCaa immediately planned murder. He lured Gavin to the ruins of Boleskine House, and the setting probably appealed to a man of Gavin's kinks. And shortly before we got there, MacCaa stabbed Gavin."

We later learned from MacCaa's confession that Sanna had gotten it a bit wrong. Apparently it had been in the newspapers that the local authorities had confiscated a large quantity of smutty materials recently, and in exchange for his silence, Gavin wanted MacCaa to take a substantial amount of the printed matter in question out of the evidence room and give it to him. I was correct in believing that Gavin had witnessed MacCaa transporting the bodies to the shed, but he was not on an innocent stroll – he was actually in the woods with two members of the manor's staff, though I won't go into the details of their assignation here.

Believe me, we'll all be happier for my circumspection on that point. Just trust me on that, please.

"Wait a minute," Stetson interjected. "I know that he let the two of you go after finding the bodies in your car because he didn't want you to be a distraction in his feud against the Hunniraubes, but what about us? Why did he have me and Cian taken away for questioning?"

"I don't think he wanted you seriously charged with murder or to damage your reputations, but I believe that he was planning to plant some more incriminating evidence at the manor against Lord Hunniraube – and Philly too, as he wanted to humiliate the whole family, and he was now planning to use the Peerage Maker scheme to discredit her. The staff and guests were mostly gone, and he wanted you two out of the way for a few hours, just long enough for him to finish his plans. I'm pretty sure that Gavin didn't text you to come to Boleskine House himself. Either MacCaa got him to unlock his phone before killing him, or he used Gavin's thumbprint when he was still warm, or maybe a dead person's head still works for facial recognition, I don't know. Anyway, something like that. He planted that letter just to justify the arrest. Then MacCaa wrote to you two, calculating that you'd find the body, but never dreaming you'd bring the four of us along. Like we said, MacCaa wasn't very skilled at thinking of alternative eventualities that might have disrupted his carefully thought-out plans. I expect that he'd have done something to frame Lord Hunniraube for that murder, and then he would have let the two of you free. In any case, he was starting to unravel. He must have just learned that his son had confessed to moving the bodies, and now he was furious at his estranged progeny for inadvertently messing up his plans, and he was also worried about what would happen to his son. He didn't want Lachlan to go to jail for something he'd done himself. He was at a loss for what to do, and I believe he wasn't behaving with the strictest standards for rationality."

"But what happened to Daddy?" Philly asked.

"I'm pretty sure he kidnapped him and is currently holding him somewhere. He planned to 'discover' him later tonight, almost certainly with incriminating evidence planted on him, and make an arrest. I don't know where, but I suspect MacCaa is holding Lord H. at his house or some isolated location. But don't worry, Philly. I don't think MacCaa did anything to harm him. I believe he wanted him safe and unhurt so he could live the rest of his life in shame and scandal. The police are probably looking for him right now, and I'm fairly certain he'll be all right physically."

"You know, MacCaa really didn't think too far ahead," Sanna noted. "He should have known that his true identity would have come out at some point during the trial, and that would have undone all of his dirty work."

"Who says there would have been a trial?" I countered. "I bet MacCaa was betting that Lord Hunniraube would simply have been placed in some mental institution without much fuss. The authorities would want everything handled quickly and without much fuss. And then after Lord Hunniraube was locked away, and Philly was suspected of being the brains behind the Peerage Maker scam, and Lachlan was most likely in charge of the manor and profiting from running it, 'Griogair' would take retirement and quietly slip away."

"I suppose that's possible," Sanna conceded.

"And then thanks to Sanna's name-dropping, MacCaa found out about me and bopped me one,"

Abhorson said with discernable annoyance, though I wasn't sure if it was directed towards Sanna, MacCaa, or both.

"Thankfully he was interrupted before he killed you. I bet he'd planned to take his weapon back with him and put Lord Hunniraube's fingerprints on it, but when he was startled, he dropped the bottle."

"How did he track you down on the boat?" Cian asked.

"I suspect that the police were keeping an eye on us, and one of them saw us renting the boat and reported back to the ersatz chief constable. He could've guessed where we were going or seen us from somewhere, and he quickly grabbed a boat and came after us. Again, that wasn't the smartest move, but he was desperate and not thinking especially clearly. I've no idea how he planned to get away with that, or how he'd explain it. After all, all the other suspects would be under police supervision, and if we'd been killed or even temporarily marooned, it would be pretty obvious that the attack on us was connected to the case. Again, he doesn't appear to be a particularly rational fellow right now. I strongly suspect that his mental state is pretty fragile. I suspect it's been wearing down for years, what with all of his obsessing over all the wrongs he's felt have been done to him. Anyway, he abandoned all logic and prudence and tried to sink our boat, but still, he should have realized how unlikely it was that he'd be able to kill all of us."

"I saw that video," Stetson said. "That was some pretty nice action work there, Miss Sanna. Would you be interested in a career change? Going into stunt work and action film acting? I've got a bit part coming up in the next Ted Testosterone movie that'd be perfect for you."

"Hard pass," Sanna said with a laugh. "I've seen too much of the seedy underbelly of Hollywood through my work in entertainment law to want anything to do with being in front of the cameras. Besides, I'm not a fan of action movies, anyway."

"What have you got against the genre?" Stetson inquired.

"There are three things that put me off a movie immediately," Sanna replied. "Constant gunfire, vulgar profanity, and Anne Hathaway."

Stetson chuckled. "Well, the Ted Testosterone films only have one of those. In any event, if any of you are ever in my corner of Texas, you all have a pace to stay."

"So what now?" Philly changed the subject. "What happens next?"

"I think we just have to wait for a bit while the police work on their investigation. I corresponded with our old friend Inspector Dankworth not too long ago, as he was an old friend of the real Griogair. He confirmed that the man we knew as Griogair was an imposter, so he'll be arriving in Inverness late tonight to do his bit to get justice for a late pal.

In the meantime, I'm sure they're looking everywhere for Lord Hunniraube. Hopefully they'll find your father very soon."

As it turned out, we only had another half hour's wait before we received news on that front. Lord Hunniraube was found alive and relatively unharmed in the basement loo of the house that MacCaa had rented as his home, though he was bound and gagged and in great discomfort. The ordeal did little to improve his disposition, but then a miracle happened. Once Zabel and Jasper's videos on our recent adventures went viral, Lord Hunniraube's backstory became public knowledge. A young woman from the east coast of Scotland wrote to us, telling us that she was an aspiring marine biologist. A couple of years earlier, she had been on a research field trip to Loch Ness, and she'd found a turtle with markings on its shell that resembled a sword. Apparently Kendrew had survived the incident from so long ago, and had been living quietly in Loch Ness for years. She'd developed a fondness for the little reptile, and had adopted him. The possibility that the little guy had ever been a nobleman's pet had never crossed her mind. She was about to move to Canada for a year-long position at a university, and she graciously returned Kendrew to Lord Hunniraube.

The effects on the nobleman were dramatic. The moment he realized that the Loch Ness Monster had not actually eaten Kendrew, all antipathy vanished and he no longer felt any desire to slay the beast. It would be an exaggeration to say that Lord Hunniraube's behavior ever became anything approaching totally conventional, but instead of spending all of his time and money targeting Nessie, he preferred to devote his energy to enjoying precious moments with his beloved turtle. His daughter approved of the change in him.

It wasn't just being reunited with his turtle that caused a dramatic shift in Lord Hunniraube's behavior. I remembered an offhand remark Philly had made about her father's nurse needing to renew his prescription for beta blockers. A while back, a colleague of my father's joined my family at dinner, and he mentioned how one of his patients had started taking beta blockers and started having adverse side effects – he started behaving erratically, and had even been diagnosed with a form of psychosis before the doctors checked his medications and realized that he might be reacting negatively to the beta blockers. Acting on my suggestion, she spoke to his general practitioner, who immediately revised his prescriptions. After a couple of weeks, there was a noticeable improvement in his condition. I suppose it was a combination of the pharmacology and the animal companion that helped him.

Incidentally, the fifty pounds of sardines (it turned out to be pounds in terms of weight, not money) were delivered the day after Kendrew was returned to Lord Hunniraube. As he no longer wanted Nessie caught and stuffed, the sardines were donated to a local charity and served on toast to those in need several days. There's no record of any of the needy recipients expressing their gratitude. Philly cancelled the hot air balloon rental, though they kept her father's deposit.

Philly continued to run Hunniraube Manor as a conference center, though there was a substantial decline in enrollment for the would-be writers' retreats. She had the idea of starting a series of mystery weekends, where actors played suspects and victims and the guests tried to solve the crimes. These proved far *more* popular, and Philly's hired me to write scenarios for these mysteries. It's proven profitable for both of us.

Waldroup resigned from the police force and started working alongside Philly at the manor part-time. During the rest of his spare hours, he pursued his dreams of YouTubing and podcasting. To date, all of his efforts have been singularly unsuccessful. On a happier note, Philly and Waldroup got married a couple of months after the end of the case, and as of this writing, they're expecting their first child.

Abhorson decided to resume his acting career, and he became a fan favourite for his various roles at the Hunniraube Manor mystery weekends. After a few months, he got a job in London drawing upon his work at The Maroon Unicorn, playing the lead role in *Faulty Towers: The Dining Experience*, an interactive dinner theatre production inspired by the classic Britcom, though I'm not exactly sure why they spell it with a "u" instead of a "w." Some sort of legal reason, I expect. The four of us attended one night and had a great time, aside from when a bowl of broccoli supergreen soup got spilled all over Jasper. As a result, the experience has soured him against all vegetables.

The latest movie based on one of Stetson's books, *The Neverending Car Chase*, was loathed by critics but beloved by audiences. As soon as he got home to Texas, he sent us an enormous box of assorted Buc-ees snacks, including twelve kinds of jerky, fudge, gummy candy, a spicy cracker dubbed a "Sizzling Saltine," pralines, and something called "Beaver Nuggets," which are little round corn puffs coated in caramel and brown sugar. Jasper went through all the bags of Beaver Nuggets in less than an hour, found out how to order them online, and without an ounce of shame, he refers to them as his "new addiction," alongside Irn-Bru.

Cian's play *The Castrator of Sevenmilelane* was a modest success, and the producers are planning a transfer to New York City. *Dame and Dibble* continues to be very popular as well. He is currently working on the book for a low-budget stage parody of all of Andrew Lloyd Webber's combined musicals.

Lachlan pled guilty to some sort of infraction regarding disposal of human remains, and he received a suspended sentence. Philly's still quite fond of her uncle, and she didn't bear a grudge towards him for moving the bodies, and she offered him his old job back. He declined, and he is now managing an inexpensive bed and breakfast in Fortrose, several miles away. Every few weeks, Philly calls him and asks him to come back. She believes that one of these days he will accept her offer.

The ersatz Chief Constable Griogair had a breakdown prior to his trial, and is now receiving excellent care at a mental hospital in northern Scotland. The doctors think that his rapid decline was due to the failure of his plans. So I realize that my friends and I are to a certain extent responsible for his poor condition, but to quote Sherlock Holmes in "The Speckled Band," "I cannot say that it is likely to weigh very heavily upon my conscience."

The estates of the Monster Hunterz sold the business to some up-and-coming YouTubers, and now the channel continues under new management. Their last video took them to northern Wisconsin, where they sought out a massive fanged creature known as the Hodag.

Zabel and Jasper's YouTube videos on the case were massive hits. Lachlan couldn't afford to replace her car, but as it turns out, there is a small but surprisingly affluent subset of the population with an interest in owning homes where terrible crimes occurred, and similarly, they have an interest in buying cars that have been comparably marred by murder. Zabel made enough off the sale not only to buy a brand-new car, but also to cover all of the expenses racked up over the course of our trip, with plenty left over to go in the bank. Sanna found another job, though the pay was a bit lower than at her previous job. Much to her chagrin, Jasper's viewers embraced her with open arms, and despite her horror at the prospect, she discovered that her share of the profits stemming from guest appearing in

Jasper's livestreams and videos was enough to make up for her decrease in salary. Her rants on various popular culture trends she hates have earned her a loyal fanbase, and thanks to her help, Jasper's subscriber numbers have exceeded two and a half million.

As for me, I continued answering Sherlock Holmes' letters at the bank, and with all the publicity from the Loch Ness case, my workload has doubled. Zabel and I are still doing great, though increasingly, Jasper and Sanna have joined in on our true crime research. We've really become an investigative team, and I have to say that I'm really enjoying our collaborative efforts.

But to conclude this narrative, I think I need to turn to our trip home to London. The four of us were in a train compartment, Jasper was reveling in his latest discovery of Scottish culinary innovations: deep fried pizza. It's exactly what it sounds like– a pizza dunked into boiling oil and served to customers who believe that their arteries could stand to be much more clogged. That last comment originated from Sanna, as might be expected. I was telling my friends my thoughts on what might happen to the recently rediscovered Nessie prop from *The Private Life of Sherlock Holmes*.

I was interrupted by my mobile ringing. "Mum?"

"I just saw you on the news! What have you been doing up there?"

I spent a little time explaining the resolution of the case to Mum, prudently excising the bit where Sanna and I leapt from the boat to attack the killer. Even though the situation was resolved and we were unharmed, Mum would freak out if she heard about it. However, a day later, after a friend saw Jasper's video and forwarded it to Mum, my prudence was undone. Just as I finished bringing Mum up to speed, I remembered that she'd been holding back on me lately.

"When will you be able to tell me what's going on with you and Dad?"

"Oh, that! I can tell you now– we've gotten the all clear, and it's all right to tell you. I need to call your siblings after I tell you. You can tell Zabel and the others, but don't go spreading it around. It's no longer a *total* secret, but it's still not to be to be shared with the general public."

And so, Mum explained the situation to me, and just a minute and a half later, I was both excited and repressing waves of laughter. After I thanked Mum for telling me and said goodbye, the giggles came out loud and powerful, and my friends waited patiently for about three seconds before poking me and demanding that I tell them just what the heck my parents had been keeping from me.

"It's all good news, really," I told them. "But I must ask all of you to promise not to say anything about it for a bit until I'm sure it's safe to make it public."

After they agreed, I explained, "My Dad's being knighted. And they're giving him some other award, too – the Order of Something Mum Couldn't Recall."

The others whooped with joy and congratulations. "For what exactly?" Jasper asked, once the initial excitement had worn away.

"Well, as you know, my Dad is a very well-respected proctologist. He's great at his job, and I don't think that there's a single prolapsed anus in all of Great Britain that he can't vanquish. But when you specialize in that field, you see a lot of things no human being should ever have to see, and you can become privy to a lot of awkward situations that, much to the relief of the people involved, are protected by doctor-patient confidentiality.

Well, Dad's built up quite the reputation, and a couple of months ago, just as he was about to leave the hospital and go home for the night, he was approached by a pair of very intimidating men in well-cut suits, and was told in the most politely threatening way possible to come with them. He was bundled off in a car with tinted windows, so he couldn't see out of them. When he arrived at the destination, he was blindfolded and led into the house. When they finally able to see again, he was stunned to see that he was in the presence of an extremely prominent member of… the Royal Family."

I had their attention before, but now they were hooked. "Which one?' Zabel asked.

"I don't know. Mum claims Dad can't tell her, but from the quaver in her voice, I'm pretty sure that she knows. She just can't say."

Sanna immediately blurted out who she believed it was, and Jasper followed with his own theory. "I can't confirm or refute your theories, you know that. But apparently this prominent member of the Royal Family had gotten into an extremely delicate situation. The precise details behind it weren't shared with me, but Mum's quite certain that if the facts of the case were to be leaked to the press, the ensuing scandal would have the potential to bring down the monarchy."

"I cannot *wait* to see this made into an episode of *The Crown*," Sanna informed me.

"Yes, well, the situation, whatever it was, turned out to be unsettlingly tricky, but Dad used his skills to resolve the situation, and all's well that ends well, at least for one royal family member's end. And now, they're so grateful, that as a reward for his proctological prowess and his discretion, he's being lavished with honours. The catch is that they're telling him that as a security measure, the ceremony has to be kept a tightly-guarded secret. Instead of the usual pomp, there's going to be a private ceremony in a room at one of the less prominent royal residences, and if word ever gets out as to why exactly he's getting a title and a medal, they'll take everything away and throw him in the Tower of London, or at least, something along those lines. Once again, Mum says that I can tell you three the basics, but you mustn't tell anybody else. You're all invited to the ceremony, by the way."

And so, a few months later, two days before Dad was to be properly, albeit quietly honoured, I received a letter in the post with a wax seal upon it. The image stamped into the wax was so misshapen I couldn't tell what it was supposed to be. Upon opening it, the note inside read:

Dear Mr. Zhuang,

I must speak to you on behalf of a family friend. When your father receives his knighthood and award later this month, I should very much appreciate it if you and Miss Carvalho would meet with me after the ceremony. Thank you.

I don't think of myself as an individual who gets easily star-struck, but I was absolutely stunned when I saw the famous royal name at the bottom of the letter. I never thought that I'd ever receive personal correspondence from this person, and now that I had, I was not just stunned that this person even knew who I was, but also that this person wanted to meet me and perhaps thought that Zabel and I might be of help.

The day of the ceremony arrived, and due to the sensitive nature of the reasons for my father's honours, it was a very low-key affair. The ceremony was held at one of the less-well-known Royal properties, in a rather small ballroom. Only about three dozen people were in attendance aside from my family and friends, and as a few other people were being rewarded for unspecified services to Crown and country, I assumed that their achievements were equally secret. The ceremony was, quite frankly, stuffy and perfunctory. The royal personage in charge said a few words as quickly as possible, tapped shoulders with a sword with minimal enthusiasm, and disappeared seconds after the task had been completed.

Shortly after the ceremony's end, an equerry sidled up to me and requested my presence in the library. Zabel and Sanna, who were sporting new fancy hats that they would never wear again, made it clear that they were coming along. Zabel, had after all, been invited. Sanna hadn't been mentioned by name, but the equerry didn't even blink. "Yes, of course. Where is Mr. Portendorfer? His presence would be welcome as well."

We found Jasper in the next room by the refreshment table, laying waste to a tray filled with salmon puffs. He refused to leave until we'd all tried a puff, and I had to admit that they were the most impressive thing I'd seen all day. Mum was curious as to where we were all going, and with the watchful eye of the equerry on me, I assured her that this was something connected to my work at the bank.

As we entered the library, we all temporarily forgot the official protocol upon meeting the royal personage in question. This was a different royal personage from the one who had so lackadaisically overseen the ceremony. We all forgot to bow and curtsey, and due to eating too many salmon puffs in rapid succession, Jasper made the sort of noise that you really are not encouraged to make anywhere near a royal personage.

Thankfully, the royal personage didn't seem to mind a bit. "I am most grateful to all of you for coming. This is a very unusual situation, and given the connection to Sir Arthur Conan Doyle, I feel like you are the only people who can help. May I introduce you to my very dear friend, Lady Aurora Comfrey?"

We murmured our greetings to Lady Aurora, a friendly looking woman in a peach-colored dress that was covered with far more lace than was really necessary. "It's lovely to meet you all. Time is precious, so I'll come straight to the point. You're an expert on Sir Arthur Conan Doyle, aren't you, Mr. Zhuang?"

I didn't want to sound boastful, so I tried to infuse as much modesty as humanly possible into my "yes."

"That's why I want to turn to you. The police have no interest in this, and the private inquiry agents I've turned to have done nothing whatsoever to help me. But given your reputation for solving Sherlock Holmes-adjacent cases, I think you're my last, best hope."

We nodded, wondering where she was going with this. "Mr. Zhuang, are you aware that Sir Arthur Conan Doyle was really a bit of a practical joker?"

"I know of one or two anecdotes about that subject."

"Then perhaps you have heard the story of the time when Sir Arthur, out of a spirit of pure mischief, once sent twelve telegrams to a dozen prominent and supposedly respectable men. Each telegram said "ALL IS DISCOVERED – FLEE AT ONCE." One of the recipients ran away immediately upon receiving that message, and was never seen again."

I nodded. "I've heard that story, but I read that it was apocryphal. In fact, I've heard a lot of different versions of that tale. Some say one telegram was sent, others say six, and the number of people who actually vanished varies from telling to telling."

Lady Aurora nodded. "Yes, the story's mutated a lot over the decades, but I can assure you that there's a kernel of truth to it. Sir Arthur Conan Doyle really did send out telegrams with that message to several acquaintances – I don't know how many, but one of them was my great-grandfather. He received Doyle's telegram one autumn day a little over a century ago. And after reading it, he set the telegram down on the coffee table, where my great-grandmother found it later. Great-Grandfather packed a couple of bags, left the house, and was never seen again. It's been a family mystery for more than a hundred years. Why did Sir Arthur send him that message? Why did my great-grandfather leave? Where did he go? We've asked a lot of investigators to answer these questions for us over the years. We've never gotten an answer. But I know how you solved that case connected to the BBC's Great Erasure, and that affair at Loch Ness not too long ago. I know you're all busy people, but my family has wondered where our ancestor went for more than a hundred years, and we're desperate for an answer."

"Can you tell me a bit about your missing relative?" I asked. "What was his connection to Sir Arthur Conan Doyle?"

"He was on my mother's side of the family. He'd carved out a pretty respectable career for himself in academia, specializing in the plays of William Shakespeare. Sir Arthur Conan Doyle was introduced to him through mutual acquaintances, based in part on the rather unfortunate coincidence about his name."

"His name?" I made a bit of an intellectual leap, and remarkably, I landed on my feet. "If he worked at a university... Are you telling me that his name was Professor –"

"Moriarty," we both said together.

"Yes, apparently he put up with a great many jokes and comments regarding his name."

"But he wasn't a criminal mastermind, of course," Zabel said.

"No. At least, I don't think so. Actually... I don't know. If he disappeared, who knows what was going on in his life? Why did he leave? Did he leave on his own accord? Were there secrets, or was someone else behind his going missing? Could it have all been an accident? I don't know, but the shadow has hung over my family for more than a century. We've hired so many investigators over the years, but we've never talked to anybody with a thorough knowledge of Conan Doyle. You're really our last chance to find out what happened."

The royal personage nodded. "I would consider it a very great favour if you would help Lady Aurora. Even if you can't find anything, I can assure you that I will personally make certain that you are well rewarded for your time and trouble."

What else could I say but "yes?" Zabel, Sanna, and Jasper responded in an identical manner, and before we knew it, we were digging into a century-plus-old missing person's case featuring an actual individual named Professor Moriarty. I didn't think that I'd ever find out what happened, but this is one instance where I happily admit to being wrong.

As for the results of the investigation… that's another story.

Milton Keynes UK
Ingram Content Group UK Ltd.
UKHW020639080923
428296UK00013B/653